NERVE

a novel

S. R. SKELTON

S.R. Skelton

This novel is entirely a work of fiction. The names,
characters and incidents portrayed in it are the work of the
author's imagination. Any resemblance to actual persons,
living or dead, events or localities is entirely coincidental.

Published in the United States of America.
ISBN-13: 978-1511948678
ISBN-10: 1511948671

For my mother,
who found herself early in life
and, through example,
showed the rest of us
where to look.

CHAPTER ONE

SWIRLING HIPS WITH scarlet red velvet wrapped so exactly you see the ripples of her flesh undulating and swaying. Every beat of the music pulsed through her body and long black hair, her spine rotating to the music like a soft, sweet cyclone. Jesse licked his lips. He wanted to grab on. To nurse at her breasts. To fuck her.

He assessed her from his position on the edge of the crowd, six or seven half-nude male bodies thumping under the manic frenzy of a strobe light intermittently blocked his view. Was she here with friends? He couldn't see any other women around her. Maybe a gay man's friend? Maybe a date? There was, after all, a smile on her face. Do women go to gay clubs alone?

When she slipped off to the bathroom, he followed. It was Madonna-Rama night at the Splendex Club, and there was no distinction between the men's and women's restrooms. Looking around, there wasn't much distinction between the men and women, either. Gender was an option, not an obligation, at the Splendex.

She took a long piss. Maybe she was snorting coke. Jesse couldn't help but feel for the small bulge in the pocket of his black leather pants, just to make sure it was still there. A little bonus he was saving for later. Or she could be just catching her breath. Jesse knew about hiding in the stalls, temporarily trading intimacy with other people's fecal matter over the people themselves. Maybe she was in there wondering why she came out tonight. Maybe she was tripping out on the patterns of the textured sheetrock. Sometimes Jesse saw faces trapped in the paint. Or the sparkles in the cement floor. Nothing like a little fool's gold in the cement and a bit of white powder to make you feel like royalty.

Luckily, Jesse had brought some mascara, so he had a reason to stand at the mirror and wait. His plan was to casually compliment her on something. The red dress or jewelry, if she was wearing any. She'd be charmed, and possibly comment on his feather boa. Feather boas were *de rigueur* at the Madonna-Rama (or so he thought when he was getting ready; really there weren't very many around). His was made of lusciously thick black feathers with silver tinsel woven in. Jesse believed in

2

dressing for the occasion. He paid for the expensive one so he wouldn't look like a first-timer—like a straight guy going to the gay club to bag the fag hag. Which she has got to be; lesbians travel in packs, or at least in pairs. Fag hags tend to be lone vaginas in a swarm of penises pointing the other direction.

Jesse was picking some white fluff out of his boa when she (finally!) came out of the stall. She opened the door with such force that the stall door banged against the wall. A bit of a line had built up during the wait. A large person wearing black leather chaps, a blue Mohawk pointed into five spikes, and a Madonna-style cone bra grabbed the opportunity and quickly disappeared into the stall. There were four sinks, but she walked straight over to Jesse and stared at him.

"I think you're following me," she accused him, but there was a twinkle in her eye. If she were angry, there wouldn't be a twinkle. Then she turned toward the sink and started to wash her hands. Both the water and the soap were supposed to be dispensed automatically with a simple wave of the hand, but the soap dispenser just make an empty grunting sound. She reached over to Jesse's sink and tried his, her cleavage giving Jesse a come hither look as she leaned.

"Well, it was convenient of you to go to the bathroom—I was sweating in there so much that my mascara was running black tears down my cheeks," said Jesse, hoping that she thought a sketchy stalker wouldn't give her an immediate admission of stalking. He was a nice stalker. The truth is that despite the boa, the leather and the illegal substance in the small of his pocket, Jesse was probably one of the most normal, nice guys at the Splendex that night, and this irked him. Jesse had spent the past two years making every effort to shed normal, nice guy and be interesting, adventurous, slightly dangerous guy. He wanted to be sexy, he wanted to have spark, but time and time again, he felt like all he was, was him: a nice guy from Virginia who could be expected to wake up in the morning and get a job done but who would never surprise anyone. Even his conservative mother, who was down right disgusted by anything resembling punk, merely rolled her eyes when Jesse got the septum of his nose pierced. She joked with her friends about Jesse's "little city phase." No one who knew him believed that he had the ability to be wild and unpredictable over the long term.

"Next time wear waterproof," she teased then she hoisted up her skirt a few inches to reveal a lace garter encircling her thigh. It had some kind of pocket in it. She pulled out a lipstick and turned toward the mirror to apply it. Jesse felt his eyes widen. He wanted to comment on just how fucking sexy that was, but decided to stick with self-depreciation. Muscle guys can go straight for the sexual innuendos and rely upon the quality of their steaming pheromones to keep the woman from walking off in disgust. Skinny guys like Jesse must try to be funny.

"The whole reason I wore mascara was to look sophisticated. Now you tell me that I bought the wrong kind?" he said with a mock whine.

"Being sophisticated means that you have so much experience you don't need to try and look sophisticated," she replied bluntly, and then leaned over to put her lipstick back in her garter/wallet. Jesse thought about it for a minute. It was not that he was completely new to this scene. He'd been a bartender for almost two years—a straight bar, of course. But it wasn't like he hadn't seen his share of wild parties. Adam's Morgan, where the bar was, was just a hop, skip, and a jump from the gay neighborhood around DuPont Circle. Of course, he was always sober behind the bar during the parties, which is exactly why he rocketed from bus boy to lead bartender in only two years. Good ol' reliable Jesse.

Every year in DuPont Circle there was a drag race where muscular men wearing false eyelashes, high heels, and all of the other accouterments of women ranging from the garish to the obscene raced around the fountain. Despite the fact that it occurred in October and the weather was usually crappy, Jesse had made it a point to go. Not to race, but to stare. There wasn't anything like that drag race where he grew up in Virginia. When his friend, Slaven, came up with the fag hag theory (that every gay club has at least ten drunk heterosexual women who are not being hit on by anyone else) and suggested that they hit up the gay club to "see some wild shit," Jesse decided to put together his own costume.

He looked at himself in the mirror. His mean, dark eyeliner contrasted with his puppy-dog brown eyes. He was wearing a tight black T-shirt and black leather pants (that he borrowed from his friend Stacy, who's a stagehand at the local black box theater). His brown hair was fabulously spiked at 9:00 p.m. when he was getting ready in front of the mirror at home, but it looked haphazard now. You could tell it wanted to be spiky still but, after all that dancing and dry ice from the fog machines, it was barely managing to be pokey. Still, Jesse thought he'd mostly pulled off the look he was going for: sexy and just slightly androgynous.

A flushing sound emanated from the stall and the blue Mohawk person squeezed between them to wash his/her hands. When he/she leaned over, Jesse couldn't help but notice that the chaps were exposing a large portion of ass. His perfectly tanned, hairless ass. Or hers. It could be a girl ass. Jesse forced himself to look away quickly; to address himself only toward the human in the room he knew for sure was female.

"Well, what I lack in experience, I make up for in enthusiasm. Dance with me." He reached out to take her hand, but she held back. Did she see him staring at the beautiful androgynous ass? How could she blame him for that? She was probably staring at it, too.

"I came to a gay club to avoid being picked up," she said, but Jesse could tell by her tone that he had already won. It was amazing how even in this modern era, so many woman couch their "yes" in the words of a "no." Jesse had never come anywhere close to doing anything a woman didn't want him to do; he had a sister to think about, and, frankly, his appetite usually ran toward women with larger jean sizes than him, so he wouldn't get very far even if he did try to push. But in the four years since a certain Tanya Jones, with her beautiful round, black tits, showed him his first real taste of Southern hospitality, Jesse had heard more no-yeses then he could count. He picked up this girl's hands again and looked into her twinkling blue eyes. She smiled, despite herself.

"Impossible. If you really wanted to avoid straight men you wouldn't have drawn me to you with the power of that amazing smile." He pulled her slightly toward him for effect. He thought he'd given up on humor, but she laughed.

"That's good... I can dig a cheeseball line like that. Worth a dance." Then she dropped his hands and started to walk out without him.

"Hey!" he said, and moved quickly to catch up. "I'm Jesse, what's your name?"

"Maya," she called out, but she didn't look back. Instead, she moved quickly through the crowd. He wished they were holding hands. Instead he felt like a puppy tagging along behind, although at a closer distance now than when he followed her into the bathroom. Somehow she wove deftly between the gyrating bodies. Syncing rhythmically with their movements, she gently touched their shoulders to let them know she was passing.

Jesse wasn't much bigger of a person, but he felt like a bull in a china shop behind her, stumbling over people's ever-changing feet, and generally pissing people off. He ignored the grumpy stares and the incredibly hot six-foot-something blond man who said, "What the fuck, dude?" after Jesse accidentally stepped on his toes. Finally, she found a place in the crowd that suited her and he caught up.

Dancing with her was a game of cat and mouse. Moving toward each other seductively, and then swirling away at the last moment. Big grins erupted across both their faces, and then she pulled hers into mock seriousness, as if she were taking some tango class and needed to flair her nose as she turned. Suddenly, Jesse felt the unmistakable hardness of a male body pushing up against his back. Maya laughed and moved closer to his front. The bass pounded, the lights twirled, the three bodies fell into perfect sync, and Jesse felt deliriously intoxicated, his heart pounding fast from the heady mixture of drugs and lust. This moment was exactly what he wanted, why he came out that night, why he moved to the city in the first place.

Later, when Jesse bought Maya a drink, vanilla vodka and Coke (not vanilla Coke and vodka), Maya explained that she came to the Splendex because she loves to dig deep into the crowd, alone. She aims for a spot right in the middle, thick with throbbing, sweating, half-dressed, horny, *gay* men, where she can suck in the flavor of their testosterone-laced pheromones without giving anything in return. Without any of them after her attention, she was free to dance in the typhoon.

Jesse loved to dig into the crowd too, but for a different reason. He couldn't help but think of that hard body that had shared a dance with them. Jesse had been too overcome to turn around and get a look at the mystery man. In fact, he had been so nervous he purposely did not turn around, and whoever it was moved on during the next song. Jesse glanced over at the masses of undulating male bodies and a jolt of fear shivered down his spine. The hard cock that had only minutes ago been pressed firmly against his ass could belong to any of them.

"It isn't safe to be alone here," Jesse told Maya, not exactly sure whether he meant it wasn't safe for her, or it wasn't safe for him. They were sitting on a couch in a corner of the warehouse that was set up as a lounge bar. The couch had a sort of sexy club vibe because it was covered in red velvet, but neither of them would have agreed to sit on its crusty, stained cushions if they could see it in the daylight. From the couch there was a good view of the dance floor. Jesse had sat on the couch before. Sitting on the edge of party, people watching, ideally with someone who enjoyed a bit of snide wit, was Jesse's usual habit at clubs, if he wasn't hiding in the thick of the dance floor. "We should stick together," he said.

"But that is the nature of men—always wanting monogamy," Maya said, as if they were mid-conversation on the topic and rolled her eyes while faking a yawn. Her black hair, which fell in at least two-foot waves down her back, caught the pulsing club light as if it contained a multitude of fireflies. Her eyelashes were equally black, which made her light eyes look as large as one of the baby dolls Jesse's sister had when they were children. Maya's full figure gave the impression of boundless offerings and her dress, crushed velvet a few shades closer to blood than the red of the couch, highlighted the best parts. Maya was absolutely luscious, and Jesse decided that she was right: he wanted her for himself.

"I have to disagree with you. It's men that don't want to be held down. Women want monogamy like mold wants bread," Jesse said, purposefully catching her eyes so she could see the corners of his crinkle, hoping the tease worked. Maya clearly wanted a little repartee.

"Oh, I agree with you about men not wanting to be tied down. My point is that they *always* want the woman to be monogamous—it has nothing to do with their own monogamy," she clarified, and then winked at him. Jesse was impressed. He couldn't wink. And he liked smart women.

"So you're into open relationships?" he teased. Jesse doubted that there was a woman on this planet who was truly cool with open relationships.

"If I'm not in love with you, I don't care who you

fuck," Maya stated emphatically. Jesse stood corrected, but not convinced. He considered responding with an argument, but she had left him an opening for seduction he couldn't resist.

"And if you were in love with me?" he asked, batting his eyes at her and trying to look adorable. Jesse loved love. Falling in love was something that Jesse did very well, and with some frequency. Relationships were so much more interesting if you were madly in love with each other. Jesse had done his fair share of "friends with benefits" and "booty calls," but he much preferred the heart-throbbing thrill of sex with the new love of his life, at least for a couple of weeks until he met someone else. Maybe Maya would be his new love.

"Don't get ahead of yourself, mascara-boy. I don't even know if you like long walks on the beach." Maya laughed. Jesse could see she was charmed. Her laugh was pure helium, floating them far above the noise of the club.

"I do love a long beach walk—I'm headed for one right now in fact. Join me?" Jesse said, quickly trying to think of a plan as he spoke. He had the keys to Slaven's car in his pocket. Slaven was the type of friend who would take a taxi home if you really needed him to, so long as you paid him properly.

"It's 4:00 a.m.!" she protested.

"Perfect. We'll be there by sunrise," he said, getting up to leave. He turned back to her, trying to give her a conspiratorial smile, and felt relieved as her eyes slowly lit up.

"You're on!" She laughed again.

"Drink for the road?" Jesse reached for his wallet to indicate that the drink was on him.

"It's almost breakfast time—I'll have my vanilla vodka with orange juice this time." Maya smiled.

CHAPTER TWO

JESSE TRIED TO keep his eyes open as the sun pushed its first spark above the horizon. He couldn't remember if the green flash was supposed to happen at the moment of sunrise, or only at sunset. He'd always wanted to see it, but today his efforts were rewarded only with burned retinas and black splotches blocking his vision. It probably didn't exist anyway, just a worldwide myth that backpacking travelers propagate to impress each other.

"The green flash was really fantastic on the beach in Bali," some ruddy, whiskered, twenty-six-year-old seen-it-all will say.

"Oh really? I have to say that my best green flash was the time I climbed the Tikal ruins in Guatemala," another will respond, his perfectly battered been-through-it-all backpack hanging off one shoulder.

The green flash competition was just as intense as the contest over who could bring home the best black and white photo of a skinny brown child, preferably with tear-stained face, or laughing while playing kickball in a swirl of dust. Not that Jesse had done a ton of traveling. Other than hitchhiking down to the Bonnaroo Festival in Tennessee last summer, he'd mostly been the friend who looked at the photos.

He did spend a large chunk of his free time the previous month hanging around at the international hostel in DC with Slaven because Slaven swore European chicks were into anal sex. It protected their virginity or something. It actually worked out for Slaven; at least Slaven claimed it did, but the only assholes Jesse got to see were a couple Israeli and Australian guys bragging about their green flash experiences.

Maya wasn't watching the sunrise anymore. Her attention had turned to a middle-aged black man sitting on the sidewalk berm playing a xylophone. Or maybe it was a small marimba, Jesse couldn't tell. His simple, rhythmic thunking on the small wooden instrument had provided the perfect sunrise soundtrack. Jesse reached for his wallet. He believed in paying people who play music for him. His mom,

Pam, had force fed him an appreciation for musicians. She used to drag Jesse and his sister all the way into DC to watch free concerts at the Kennedy Center, and every Thursday for years she'd dropped them off at Mrs. Shilling's cramped old house for piano lessons. He can still remember the ache in his stomach when he had to admit that he didn't practice, again. Mrs. Shilling always smelled like she smoked cigarettes that had gone bad. Like she bought them forty years ago, along with the rest of the over-stuffed furniture, oriental rugs, and bric-a-brac whatnots that cluttered every corner of her house. Jesse had whined and complained about going every time without fail. By the time he was eleven he refused to practice, not just because it was tedious, but also to make a point about how much he detested it. His poor mother had finally let him quit after he humiliated her right outside Mrs. Shilling's house, screaming that he hated piano, Mrs. Shilling's stinky old lady breath, and any kind of music that was ever played by an orchestra.

Jesse felt a reflexive cringe of embarrassment every time he remembered it. Not that Pam was one to give into temper tantrums. Years later Jesse realized that she had let him quit because it was clear that he was as far from a prodigy as a child could get. That had nothing to do with obstinacy, it was just a sad fact. Jesse could probably still pump out most of Beethoven's "Für Elise" if someone's life depended on it, but he was not musical. Not even rhythmic, unfortunately. Part of the reason why he liked to dig into the dance floor at clubs was because it was too dark and crowded in there for anyone to notice that he was off-beat.

But, the piano lessons had done some good, Jesse recognized it now; they had given him just enough of a peek into the music world to be impressed by the people who stuck with it. And if the musician gave Jesse the impression of years of practice, of a single mother who used her precious dollars to pay for music lessons for an insolent child, Jesse was willing to dig into his pocket, pull out a buck, and pay for it.

"If I could wave a magic wand and suddenly play any instrument, it would be either a violin or a saxophone. Those are hands-down the best street corner instruments," Jesse said to Maya. Over the years he'd thought about trying a different instrument; maybe piano just wasn't his thing. But he just didn't have the self-motivation to do anything more than what was assigned to him.

Despite that one torrential outburst when he was eleven, Jesse was very good about doing as he was told and little else. If teachers or bosses asked for something to get done, it would, but Jesse's personal goals fell by the wayside. He didn't eat right, he didn't exercise much and he definitely didn't make time to learn an instrument. It wasn't entirely his fault, he reasoned. Millennium kids got so many enthusiastic compliments for just being cute couch potatoes that they had no patience for the basic drudgery of acquiring complicated skills. Everyone knew that. It was all over the Internet. It was the parents' fault for building up their children's self-esteem so well that they felt absolutely perfect just the way they were, no improvements needed.

Jesse looked at Maya. She didn't seem to fall into that mold. On the drive to the coast last night she'd told him that she was on scholarship at Georgetown. The first member of her family to go to college. And she was totally self-motivated. She said her parents don't really get why she was here. They were hippies who couldn't care less if she graduated with honors from Georgetown, or moved to an ashram in India; she joked that they'd probably prefer the latter. Her childhood sounded amazing. She had lived all over California and Hawaii, mostly in places she described as "cooperatives." She had traveled everywhere with her parents, too. All over India and Asia. It sounded like a fairytale to Jesse, who had grown up in the suburbs outside of DC. He kept asking her questions, but when they pulled into the parking lot she turned to him and told him to "shut the fuck up." Then she unzipped his pants and gave him the best blow job he'd ever had. Even now, his dick was throbbing again just thinking about it.

"What are you thinking about?" he asked her, feeling a little cliché, and hoping he wasn't spoiling her sunrise reverie. She hadn't responded to his musical instrument musings.

"My kid," she said somewhat nonchalantly, but she knew she had just lightly tossed an anvil into the conversation, and the weight of it made her stand up. Jesse stood up too, and they started to walk together down the boardwalk.

"You have a child?" He was a little incredulous. Maya couldn't be more than 22 years old.

"She's three. I had her when I was 17, and she is being raised by the father's parents," she said, answering the obvious questions Jesse hadn't yet asked. She climbed up on the handrail and started walking it with her arms out, like on a tightrope, as if physical distance from Jesse would underscore how different her life was from his. For a moment Jesse tried to imagine what it would be like to know you have a child somewhere out there in the world, but failed. Jesse didn't have any experience with children and, quite frankly, had probably gone years without interacting with or even thinking about one. Working in bars all night and sleeping till 3:00 p.m., Jesse inhabited the opposite side of the clock. He looked up at Maya and placed the information about her child in the same category as the fact that she'd spent her sixth-grade year traveling around Thailand. It was all utterly exotic.

"Do you visit her?" he asked, as he almost stepped on some freshly chewed day-glow green gum. Why do people just spit gum out on the sidewalk? Was every circular stain on the sidewalk from gum? If so, gum stains on cement either last forever, or gum spitting had become an epidemic. The sidewalk was covered with gum-sized round, oily stains.

"No, it's really weird. I think about her a lot,

especially when it's her birthday, or Christmas. I wonder if she's happy, and I hope she's getting fun presents. I want to buy one for her, but I feel too guilty that I can't take care of her. I'm sure the last thing she wants is some plastic toy from the mom that doesn't give her love. I hope her dad's parents are treating her like a princess. They promised me they would..."

"Are you allowed to visit?" Jesse asked.

As the sun rose, a flush of cold air suddenly pushed off the ocean—maybe the warming air off the coast was pushing a cool breeze onto shore. Maya's nipples reacted, and her thin dress did little to hide their erection. Jesse tried to focus on the hard reality that this girl had a child, but his mind started drifting to the way she looked a few moments ago, sucking like a fiend.

Maya jumped off the wall and suddenly looked distracted. Just as Jesse was about to break the silence and maybe change the subject to something more comfortable, maybe talk her into going back to the car, she turned and looked straight at him, as if to gauge whether he was a trustworthy vessel for her to pour her secrets into.

"I guess so," she replied. "Technically it was an open adoption. I did visit once when she was about three months old, but it felt really awkward. The baby didn't know me, of course, and she cried most of the time I was there. I didn't know how to soothe her, so I handed her back to her adopted mom."

"Babies cry a lot, it probably had nothing to do

with you," Jesse offered. The only thing he knew about babies was that when he used to be a waiter he hated getting the tables with babies. The crying and mess was often inversely proportional to the tip.

"Maybe. I thought she was angry with me for being so inadequate. She was yelling at me to go away already and just leave her in peace with her new family..." Maya's voice drifted off.

Instinctively Jesse wanted to calm her, to say that she was wrong, and a baby couldn't possibly think all that. But his best friend Jimmy growing up had been adopted, and one night when they were around twelve years old they'd climbed up into Jesse's attic to look for treasures. When he found his old baby photo album Jimmy told him that if he ever saw his birth parents he would run away because they were such losers. Then Jimmy punched the wall, leaving three little indents in the sheetrock where his knuckles had landed. Jesse was surprised at his friend's anger but, because even at twelve Jesse was already well on his way to being the overly empathic, overly analytical person he was now, he realized that his friend was using anger to cover up sadness.

"I guess I can imagine an adopted child feeling that way toward a birth mom, but probably deep down inside adopted kids just want to believe that their birth mothers loved them. Loved them so much they found parents who would raise them in the best possible way." Jimmy's adoptive parents were great. His dad had coached their little league team a few years, and his mom seemed to always be making cookies. And he had two of them, which was twice the number of parents that Jesse had the privilege of enjoying.

"I got to know the adopted parents a bit during the pregnancy. They were sweet to me. After they found out that their son knocked me up they called and asked if they could talk to me before I went in for my abortion. I hadn't made an appointment yet, but I'd told the father I had. Really, I was still trying to get a grip on what was happening. I only barely knew the father... he was a grade younger than me, but he was a smooth talker who introduced me to a half-pint of tequila and the bench seat of his friend's truck at a school dance. Not that I was totally innocent. I think I taught him the Jose Cuervo song." She admitted. Then explained, "I had just turned 17, and I thought I was ready for fun.

"When I went to lunch with his parents, I was first surprised at how young they looked. Definitely younger than my parents. It turned out that they had gotten married when *she* got pregnant at 18. Then for some reason she didn't have any more children. They were cute together—laughing a lot, and finishing each other's sentences. I misunderstood what they wanted at first, and told them that I couldn't possibly get married at 17. But then they just came out with it and suggested that they take the baby. They'd obviously planned to ask me, because they had all sorts of ideas. They offered to pay to transfer me to another school during the pregnancy if I wanted to get away. They even mentioned a few really expensive private schools."

"What did your parents say?" Jesse asked. He had no idea what his mother would have done if his sister had gotten pregnant in high school. Except freak out. She would have totally freaked out.

"My dad was against it. He wanted me to get an abortion and be done with it. Move on with my life. But Mom felt more understanding when I told her that I didn't want to kill the baby. Growing up, Dad expressed opinions, but Mom called the shots, so that was that.

"Really, I had to make a quick decision at that point, because by the time I figured out I was pregnant I was nine weeks, and you're supposed to get it done before twelve weeks. I just kept thinking that the baby might be happy with these people; they were family. In some cultures the grandparents care for the children while the parents work the fields or whatever, right?"

"In Micronesia the grandparents have a right to claim the firstborn grandchild for themselves," Jesse said.

"Really?"

"I read it somewhere."

"So it must be true!" She winked at him and laughed, and then pointed to a flock of pelicans surfing the waves. Her nails were painted black with silver z's on them. Or maybe they were lightning bolts. Fingernails are windows not to the soul, but to the mind. Hers were clean, cared for, and generally unworried. Jesse's were bitten down to the nubs. Was it technically cannibalism when you bite your nails? What about that little bit of dried skin that forms around the nail? Of course, Jesse thought, it was insecurity that drove his hand-mouth habit. Somewhere he heard that active minds have to have a body movement like tapping, doodling, or chewing gum, in order to focus properly. His mind clearly required a certain amount of self-cannibalism to whirl and tick.

"Did you go to another school?" he asked, wanting to find out what happened. What a crazy story. Not for the first time, Jesse congratulated himself on being born a boy. Growing up in a predominantly female household had given him first-hand knowledge that bodies that don't have the responsibility of looking pretty while bleeding were easier to live in.

"No, I toughed it out with a few really great friends. I was chubby, with frizzy hair, living in a beach town full of blond girls in bikinis. I really wasn't in the running for prom queen anyway."

"All the best-looking college girls were chubby in high school. Why is that?" Jesse asked, catching her eye and offering a smile to go with the compliment.

"I think you just like a woman with ass," she flirted, wiggling and then twirling her beautiful rear just out of reach of his now-outstretched arms. She had the confident tone and body language of a woman who knew when a man was wrapped around her finger. Women can smell your desire like a wolf can smell your fear, Jesse reminded himself.

Jesse looked around to see if there were any nooks he could pull her into. Some private corner where they could continue this conversion about her ass. But her eyes had grown distant again, and he could tell that the only way to get this woman back in the mood was to continue listening. Not that there could be much more to the story. He already knew the important part: she gave the baby away, for better *and* for worse. Except, there was one thing.

"What is her name?" he asked.

"They named her Sienna Mckenzie. I had sort of wanted to give her a flower name, like Lily or Violet, but I didn't really know if I had a right to tell them, and they seemed really excited about the way Sienna Mckenzie flowed off the tongue when they asked me if I liked it. I guess there is a river somewhere in Oregon called Mckenzie where they went fly-fishing once. 'Sienna' is actually getting to be a popular girl's name nowadays. When she was a baby they called her 'Mattie-Cakes,' but I don't know if they do anymore..."

Her gaze retreated inside and her words drifted off. Suddenly, Jesse felt a tremendous tenderness toward her. She was still a child herself, really. He wanted to protect her, to fix this unfixable problem.

"Where is she?" he asked, his mind whirling, brainstorming for solutions.

"What do you mean?"

"Does she live nearby?"

"Oh, no, she's still in California; Santa Cruz. After

I had the baby, my parents moved us to Peru. I finished high school at an international school, and then moved out here for college. You know, the other day I was talking to a girl in my water aerobics class, and she mentioned living in family housing with her son. I had no idea that some universities have family housing. She has a kitchen and everything. I looked it up on the Internet, and some universities even have free daycare. I always thought that keeping a baby would make college impossible and generally ruin your life, but she looked great."

"My mom works at a junior college in Virginia that has access to family housing, too. But, I totally know what you mean, though, I've been living my life under the assumption that babies are gremlins that will turn all of my dreams inside out." Jesse started to pull out his wallet to show her the condom he kept there at all times, but he didn't. She hadn't laughed at his joke about baby-gremlins. "I bet things aren't so easy for that mom, and she isn't 17, either," he offered; but something else had caught his attention.

Did Maya just say that she lived in Peru? Envy filled Jesse's body as he mentally added up the places Maya had mentioned so far: California, India, Asia, Peru. He tried to imagine the scenes, her as a young child casually hanging out at the Taj Mahal or Hollywood Boulevard, but instead he thought of his own mother.

Pam, wearing her 9-5 work wear from the sales

rack at Macy's, sitting behind the desk, trying to convince college kids to go easy on the loans. "If you live like a professional in college, you'll live like a student when you're a professional," she liked to say. She worked in the financial aid department of Northern Virginia Community College, near where Jesse grew up. She had never remarried after Jesse's dad died when Jesse was only a few months old. Instead, she burrowed into her role as provider for Jesse and Trish, his sister. She sold her dream house, moved them to one of those newly developed townhouse "neighborhoods" where every house was identical, enrolled them in daycare, and started a life pattern that stayed the same for over twenty years. Just like the beige row house and their typical American family: one boy, one girl, the predicable, steady rhythm of each week blended softly, one indistinguishable from the next.

When they were little, before baseball, even the missing dad did little to differentiate them, as most of the other dads in the neighborhood weren't home much anyway.

By the time he was ten, Jesse had craved something more. In high school, he had applied for a scholarship to go abroad, but a straight-A student with red, curly hair named Kevin got it. What kind of impression will America make on the world if it only sends out the nerds? Jesse's solid C+ record reflected the fact that he found school tedious and boring. Also, he wasn't worried about getting into some four-year university because he knew they couldn't afford it anyway. When things got annoying at work, Pam always joked that she had to keep her job because someday her kids were going to use that tuition discount. She voiced her expectations that her children would go to college to motivate them academically, but Jesse interpreted it as meaning that his future, like his present and past, was set in some groove pattern that was so deep and straight, anything he actually did was irrelevant.

When Trish graduated high school and enrolled at the college, she actually raved to their mom about how great it was to get the discount, as if this were some special treat instead of their birthright. Two years later, she was happily kick starting a career as a nurse, and it was Jesse's turn to sign up for more years of falling asleep at his desk. Then suddenly, someone threw him a parachute. His best friend Slaven's uncle, whose real name was something long and Polish but whom everyone called "Mr. Bob," owned a restaurant in DC and needed some servers he could trust. Although he always calculated into his projections that his servers would pocket a few bucks here and there, the skimming was starting to get out of control. Mr. Bob invited the boys to visit, and suddenly it felt like a window opened up in his world, and he could see the whirl of colors and people outside.

The restaurant was in Adam's Morgan. Adam's Morgan was considered a Latin neighborhood, and it was; but it also had the best lineup of bars you could find in the entire city. Anyone who was anyone ended up there at some point over the weekend, and Jesse had a ticket into the heart of it. At nineteen, it was his idea of heaven. He geared up a whole long list of why sewing his oats in the big city was much more educational than listening to some teacher drone on in community college, but his mom actually let him go easily. Maybe one career-bound child out of two was success enough or maybe she had anticipated that he would need a little city phase to let off some steam before he settled down.

Jesse had always been a bit of a floater, and as soon as Mr. Bob turned him on to the old Beat writers, floating with style became the goal. He sought out interesting friends, which meant that they had to fit in the category of artist, actor, tattooed, band member, or restaurant/bar employee, with very limited exceptions for extremely hot people (a.k.a. "arm candy"). He got involved in a local black box theater and pierced his nose septum with a gold hoop, like a bull.

After two years, he felt like he owned the place. He knew everyone who worked the strip. He had worked his way up from busboy to lead bartender, with a corresponding increase in both wages and sex. Every weekend the Adam's Morgan bars and clubs would fill up with university students, political interns, young lawyers, and other mainstream people out for a good time. He thought of them as tourists. Foreigners with money. Just for a laugh, sometimes he bartended Saturday nights with a faux-gay accent: "Oh, *girl,* if you don't grab this man up, I will!" The drinkers from Georgetown had no idea he was faking, but for some reason they always tipped gay Jesse better than straight Jesse. And Slaven, who worked the bar with him, actually peed his pants once trying to restrain from laughing.

But, after hearing Maya's travel stories, all of Jesse's experiences seemed small. Adam's Morgan was a hundred times more thrilling than Reston, Virginia, but it was less than 100 miles away. Simply being in Maya's sphere, he realized, could transport him into a universe where people travel. Where *he* traveled. He wanted to grab onto Maya like a kite.

"She said she had her baby her sophomore year of college," Maya admitted.

"That is a totally different situation from yours," Jesse said, trying for a consoling tone. Suddenly an idea flashed through his mind, and before he had a chance to think it through it tumbled out of his mouth. "You know, my uncle Jim in Denver has a car he said he'd give me if I made it out there. I was thinking about hitchhiking. Why don't you come with me? I could drive you to California from there." Jesse felt the thrill of possibilities unfolding before him. Just being around Maya had changed his vision! Where previously the car that his uncle offered him had seemed more like a hassle than a gift (the cost of transporting it was more than half the cost of buying a used car, and then he'd have to figure out where to park it), and he hadn't been interested enough to even consider hitchhiking to

Denver before. Now it struck him as an opportunity to get out and do something he'd been dreaming about for years: go to California.

In the United States there are two types of people: those who love California, and those who do not. For Jesse, a newly minted hedonist, California represented the freedom to follow one's cravings. The gateway to reveling in his soul, which he was certain, closely resembled Kerouac's. He imagined a big, all-night fuck-a-thon, where everyone was too busy racking up bedpost notches to keep careful tabs on the who's and whys. At one of his favorite DC clubs they would throw foam parties, where undulating people and glittering lights would mix with mounds and mounds of bubbles. Sweaty from dancing, high on whatever the Spice Man was selling that night, laughing at his friends with bubbles on their heads...these memories would no doubt keep him warm through winter nights when he was old. But, for every fantastic night in DC, there was always someone raving about how the scene in San Francisco was better. "The best clubs in the world!" guaranteed Slaven, who had a cousin over there and knew these things.

"What?! You're wild!" Her eyes sparkled, and then then dimmed. "It sounds romantic, but really, I don't think we could visit her. It would probably totally freak her out. I mean, look at me—what if she has some sort of fantasy about this fairy godmom, and then I show up with my black fingernails? Anyway, I have a summer job at the university library, and no cash."

Jesse looked at her. Her red velvet dress was showing a bit of wear, and the glitter on her eyelids from last night had mostly worn off. She looked tired, maybe not as pretty as he thought before. His buzz started fading with the sunrise, an ache in his jaw flaring up as the drugs in his system faded. But he was already giddy with anticipation over the trip, and he must convince her. The prospect of an adventure was tingling at his spirit and he needed her, like a ticket, or a crutch.

"You don't have to look motherly. You could look like a cousin or a big sister or something. I mean, she already has a mother."

Her visible flinch at the word "mother" brought Jesse back to the ground. Obviously his excitement had done temporary damage to his ability to be empathetic. He tried to repair, "I shouldn't have said that, I guess. I was just trying to take the pressure off you." Images of hitchhiking across the country with her were already swirling in his head. *O beautiful for spacious skies, For amber waves of grain, For purple mountain majesties above the fruited plain!* He sat down on a bench and pulled her down into his lap. "Just imagine, sitting in my lap in the back of some farmer's truck. Bumping along the highway through the night, under the stars." He squeezed her and looked out at the ocean, seeing only the empty highway in his mind.

"What about seatbelts, Jack?" she asked, and his heart swelled with love at the mention of the famous beat writer Jack Kerouac

Seatbelt laws had ruined the hobo fantasy for him before.

"I have a little cash, and if we run out I've heard that there are, like, millions of farms in California that just hire workers straight off the streets. I'd be the sweaty farm hand and you could be my cowgirl."

"Ha! Only a white city boy would fantasize about being a migrant worker," she teased.

"I'm not a city boy! I'm from Reston, Virginia," he corrected her. Reston was about halfway in between Dulles International Airport and Washington, DC. Outside of being one of the first planned communities in the United States back in the sixties, its main attribute was its proximity to both of those better known landmarks.

"Exactly." Maya laughed.

"Why are you pulling the race card on me? You look pretty fair yourself, sister," Jesse argued. Her hippy heritage may be 100% cooler than his suburban roots, but she was definitely still white.

"My mother is Jewish, so if you want to travel with me, you'll have to get used to the race card, the woman card, and any other card I flip in your white male face—that's the way it is, *brother*. We live in reality, or we don't live at all." Maya twisted around so he could see her point back and forth between them with her finger to emphasize the "we." Jesse decided to take this as sign that she was leaning his way on the summer plans.

"Okay, I'm game," he replied with a purposefully light tone, to manipulate the conversation into a more friendly space. Jesse loved a little light teasing if it was sexual in nature. Years of flirting across the bar had taught him that art. But otherwise, he couldn't stand conflict. His sister Trish had gone through an anti-white feminist thing her first year in collage which, as far as Jesse could tell, consisted mostly of Trish telling Jesse that everything he and their mom thought or did was wrong. She'd ruined Christmas dinner that year arguing about "white privilege." Jesse had countered that if whites had such privilege, why didn't she get a free ride to some fancy college? This was a bad move though, because Trish said that affirmative action was needed to overcome the stink of slavery still pervasive across America, and Pam got all upset because she works at a college and said she knew first-hand how badly affirmative action screwed over hard-working white children. Trish said something about how if we only educated more black women to take over the government we'd probably all be better off because everyone knew that black women were, like, totally selfless, super loving, and good at caring for everyone, while white men just embezzled government money for themselves. Then Pam yelled that if Trish didn't stop taking feminist classes she would end up a lesbian, and Trish screamed that she wished she were a lesbian, just to prove her point. Seventeen-year-old Jesse had no idea what the point was. He'd spent the evening trying to get his mother and sister to calm down.

Over the next year he figured out how to handle this new feminist Trish, and really it wasn't too far off from the best way to handle most people. If he just agreed with what she said in the moment she said it, he could easily avoid a scene without actually having to do or change anything about his life. "Give me what you got, but I think if you give me a chance you'll find that I'm pretty conscious of my inherent privileges." he said to Maya.

"Absolute power corrupts absolutely," Maya said, but Jesse's strategy had worked, and her tone had lost its bite. The tension slipping under the rug tickled his toes. Her body snuggled against his, the smell of her sweat reminding him of the dry ice at the Madonna-Rama. But last night seemed like ages ago. The sun was rising higher in the sky, shining down on this new day, this new life filled with possibilities that weren't there yesterday.

After a few moments Maya, still facing the ocean, her voice subdued, said, "You know when I first told you about Sienna I did it partially for shock value. I like shaking up people's expectations, and, really, ultimately their world views. But I've never told anyone about how I couldn't even hold her, couldn't comfort her, and haven't visited. It's not, um, not on my usual list of in-your-face subject matter. For some reason I trust you, even with my shame, in a way I haven't trusted anyone in a while."

"I can't believe that it's been less than 24 hours since we met," Jesse whispered into Maya's ear, her soft hair ticking his face.

"That's impossible," she replied. "I feel like I've known you all my life."

CHAPTER THREE

THE TELEPHONE RANG around eight in the morning on Tuesday. Jean was up, of course, because by five thirty baby "peanut" had started quite literally kicking the pee out of her and, although she did manage to make it all the way to the bathroom and back to bed without soiling herself, within twenty minutes three-year-old Sienna had entered her room, yanked at her blankets, and announced "Mommy! It's morning! Wake up! It's morning!"

Jean was making toast for Sienna and contemplating what to eat for breakfast. Not a bagel. A few weeks ago at her prenatal appointment they gave her some gawd-awful sugar drink, and then measured how her pregnant body handled the jolt. She didn't fail the test, but she got what approximates a D- and was now officially at risk for gestational diabetes. It wasn't life-threatening or anything major, but her midwife wanted her on a strict diet: No bread. No sweet fruit. No chocolate. Jean was trying her best to follow the rules but, damn, other than pickles, that list pretty much summed up her diet over the past few months. So she was hard-boiling eggs (her midwife's voice ringing in her ears: "eggs and kale: the perfect pregnancy diet") and lusting over Sienna's sourdough toast when the telephone rang.

Jean recognized Maya's voice immediately, even though they hadn't spoken in three years. She had hoped to never hear the sound of that voice again. Of course she's always known that it would happen someday, but, dear Jesus, *why now?* Jean thought, as her mind started to swirl with anxiety and dread. This was the last thing that her relationship with her daughter needed. Ever since Jean's private law practice had started ramping up a little over a year earlier she had felt torn by the fact that she wasn't spending enough time with Sienna. Sienna's daycare had an open door pick-up policy from three to five and, despite every promise she made to herself, these last few months Jean found herself consistently picking Sienna up five minutes after five, the last guilty parent to pick up the last lonely child. For Jean, deep in the trenches of client emergencies and fascinating research projects, lately five p.m. had been sneaking up like a petulant child jumping from behind the corner to scream "boo!" She would run out the door of her office, five p.m. screaming at her from her watch, open client files screaming at her from her desk, and her guilt over the fact that she had wanted to pick Sienna up early for some "special time" screaming loudest of all.

With the baby coming, it was only going to get worse. At least now Jean had bedtime, when she could read and cuddle and be the loving, focused mother she wanted her child to have – even if only for a couple hours in the evening. But soon she'd have a newborn to care for and where would that leave Sienna? Of course she had a loving father, Marvin really was a good dad, and happy to help if he wasn't teaching evening classes, but no amount of daddy love can fill the hole left by an absent mother. The fact that Sienna was adopted caused the mommy-guilt to slice even deeper than with her first child because she couldn't tell herself that she was doing the best she could under "surprise" conditions-- she had wanted Sienna, fought for her. If it wasn't for Jean, Maya probably would have aborted her, but Jean had convinced Maya. In those first weeks, when things weren't certain, Jean had prayed to Sienna's little spirit that if only she would help convince Maya, Jean would be the best mother possible. The most perfect, wonderful mother a girl could hope for.

Jean felt so panicked she couldn't focus on

Maya's words, exactly. There was something about living in DC, traveling across the country soon. Hitchhiking? Jean envisioned a big, swirly black cloud moving slowly across the United States— headed towards California. Hopefully, not all the way to California?

"Oh! That sounds like fun....Yes, I'm doing well. I'm pregnant again.... Just five more weeks.... Sienna? She's wonderful. You should see how smart she is..." Did Jean just invite her? She didn't mean to invite her. There was no sugar-coating it: Jean simply could not afford to have Sienna's bio-mom sweep in for a visit now. The work-life balance was about to get very wobbly and an appearance from Maya could easily be the swift kick that knocks the entire thing down. "But, of course, right now is a little tricky, with the baby coming and all..." she quickly added. Maya's "Oh" sounded pitiful, disappointed. A trickle of hope sprung inside Jean that the girl would hang up, move on to some other spur-of-the-moment vacation plan. But then Maya said she would stay in a hotel, just a short visit. Two or three days max. She would be gone before the baby came.

A flame of indignation roared to life inside Jean. Did Maya just presume to know when the baby will arrive? Did Maya think that her nine month detour off the usual teen highway gave her some insight into the world of babies that alluded Jean during her twenty-year hold on the title of mother? Anger welled up inside Jean where hope had dissipated, but it was too late. Maya had already hung up. She would be there in about two weeks. She'd give a call when she got close to California to give a better estimate.

Jean stood there holding the telephone in her hand. She wanted to call Maya back and tell her, more firmly, that it was not a convenient time. Baby Peanut might come early. Jean was too exhausted to have company. And, could Maya, please, get back to her own life, and let Jean get back to pretending that she doesn't exist? But it was an open adoption, damn it.

Back when Maya was pregnant with Sienna, Jean had made all sorts of promises about visits. (What a desperate fool she was!) Not that "open" means that the birth mother can just barge in whenever she wants. Does two weeks' notice count as barging in? Maybe a day or two visit wouldn't kill her, and then Maya would leave for another three years. Didn't she say she was going to college over there on the East Coast? She has got to have a few more years of that, Jean thought. Optimism knocked. Maybe Maya wouldn't make it across the country before she bored of the trip. Hitchhiking is hard. It isn't safe. She might get as far as Ohio and then fly home. Lots of kids give up and fly home. But of course, Maya grew up with those nomad parents of hers. Sleeping in ditches was probably second nature to her.

Jean's eyes focused, and she realized that she was staring at her daughter out the window. Sienna was already outside, climbing on the gym. Anyone who thought all boys were active and all girls sit around doing art projects needed to spend a day with this little girl. It was only eight twenty and she probably already had grass stains on her school clothes. "I swear these pants were clean when I put them on her this morning!" Jean would joke when she dropped the girl off at preschool. She glanced over to the pool. Marvin still hadn't finished putting the gate up. Thank goodness they'd decided to put the kitchen window overlooking the backyard when they did the remodel.

Sienna looked happy, and the bounce of her wavy black hair made Jean's heart swell, then sink. Her mind swirled with questions. What was Maya up to? What does she want, anyway? She's what, nineteen? Twenty? Probably at college somewhere. Why would a college kid want to dredge up this history? Ugh. Why do I have to deal with this now? Jean tried to calm herself. Maya can't take Sienna away. Jean had made sure of that legally. But what if she shows up and steals Sienna's heart?

Jean had never told Sienna about Maya. She was planning to be honest about the whole thing, but the girl was only three. It hadn't come up. There hadn't been any need to discuss it because, until now, things hadn't been awkward. Even the names had been easy. The cutesy names Sienna gave them when she was two had stuck. They were convenient, so the family allowed them to stick. And they worked: Sienna called Marvin "Poppy," and Jean "NuNe," names which nicely blurred the fact that they were both her legal parents and her biological grandparents. She called Maverick "Ricky," which suited him just fine. What is a name, anyway, but a way of identifying the people you love? Sienna had a family of people that loved her and, until now, Maya hadn't been a part of it. Jean wondered if she had an obligation to introduce Maya as "family" now.

When Sienna first started preschool, she hated it. She would cry every time Jean dropped her off and Jean would sit outside on the steps, away from the windows so Maya couldn't see her, and listen to her wail, while Jean's own tears dropped onto the cement. The teacher said that Jean needed to put in some effort to bridge the "attachment gap," and gave her a photo for Sienna's room. Once framed, the teacher's photo blended in with the other real relatives that occupied that shelf. Jean and Sienna would look at it at bedtime, and talk about the fun things Sienna did during the school day. And it worked. Jean tricked Sienna into believing that her teacher was part of their clan, and that made it okay to spend the day at school. Jean didn't have a photograph of Maya. Even if she did, the idea of seeing it on the shelf caused a spasm of heartburn to seize her chest. Hopefully, Maya wasn't expecting Sienna to know anything about her. There was simply no way Jean would be able to properly prepare Sienna for the visit over the next two weeks. It was better, Jean decided, to tell Maya when she called next to just play it like Maya was a friend from out of town. Just one of the many people who popped in and out of Sienna's life without rippling the waters. Sienna wouldn't remember the visit anyway after a couple of weeks; why expose her to any potential grief over a two day visit? Jean couldn't tell if she was being rational, but she felt better after making that decision.

She looked down at the stovetop. She had eaten the toast, and the eggs had been boiling for twenty minutes.

CHAPTER FOUR

"I AM SO sorry, but I forgot your name," Jean admitted to the pretty brunette who looked way too thin to have a baby that young in her sling. Maybe she was bulimic, Jean thought, and then chided herself immediately. Her preoccupation with how quickly other mothers lost their weight, not movie star mothers (she wasn't that much of a self-saboteur), but other mothers at the neighborhood playground, was her most recently acquired personality flaw. The woman's little boy had talked Sienna into a game of tag (or the three-year-old version: a disorganized chasing and whacking that, while certainly cringe-worthy, had, so far, avoided the necessity of mom intervention). The game had lasted for over five minutes, so, in accordance with playground custom, skinny-mom and Jean were now obligated to chat.

"Oh, no problem, I'm Wynn. I forgot your name, too." She smiled, then added half to herself, "I'm bad about that. I'm so self-conscious and worried about what I'm going to say when I meet someone new that I completely forget to listen to the name."

"Huh," Jean giggled, "and here I was thinking I suffered some sort of absentminded professor-syndrome—just too cerebral to remember names—when really it was insecurities all along!"

"I'm impressed! You're that pregnant, running after your daughter, and still use twenty-five cent words like 'cerebral.' I swear my boys suck all of my brain cells right out my nipples." At that moment, Jean knew she and Wynn would become friends. A mom who admits insecurities, compliments her, and talks about her nipples in the first five minutes was Jean's kind of friend, despite her pant size.

"I'm Jean. How old is your little one?" Jean asked.

"He's five months... here," she said, pulling back the rim of the sling to show Jean an angelic sleeping face. Just looking at a baby that young caused a thrill of excitement to rush through Jean's engorged body. Only eight weeks to go. The thought made Jean want to pee with joy. Of course, lately she had to pee every twenty minutes no matter what she was looking at. Jean moved on to the important question.

"So, five months and, what, four years? How far apart are they?" Jean asked, nodding to the older boy, now climbing up the twisty slide with Sienna in fast pursuit. She was well aware that her tone gave away the fact that she was desperate to know how her two would get along.

"Exactly three years apart. They had the same due date, but little Julien here came almost a week late. My Oliver was perfectly timely, except it took him almost three days to get out!" Wynn laughed, although it probably wasn't all that funny at the time.

"Ouch! I was so lucky when my oldest son was born. The labor was maybe five hours. Of course, I was seventeen then. We'll see how this thirty-eight-year-old body does."

"Oh, you'll be okay. Once the body has done it once or twice it knows what it's doing. How was your second? Jules here came flying out of me. I sat down to pee and almost had him in the toilet. My midwife joked that if she hadn't dragged me out of the bathroom I would have had an 'alternative water-birth.'"

"Sienna is adopted," Jean admitted.

"Wow, she looks exactly like you! I never would have guessed."

"She's my biological grandchild, long story; but I adopted her at birth, so she's legally my child." Gawd, Jean thought, it always sounds so daytime TV drama when she came out with it, but there wasn't any easy way to explain the fact that Sienna had her eyes.

Wynn stepped over and plopped down on a bench. Jean wondered if she knocked the poor woman down with the weight of her story. Jean sat down too, and started digging through her bag for a water bottle, mostly to avoid eye contact. She braced herself and waited for Wynn to do the mental calculation, and realize that teen pregnancy must be a Simmons family tradition.

"Even if it was a long time ago, your body will remember," Wynn said, politely avoiding nosing into the more interesting topic of Jean's messy family. Or maybe she couldn't add. "Do you have a dula? I didn't have one with Jules and I kinda regret it. If you're going with a hospital birth, it's so helpful."

"Yes, thank goodness, we finally found one we love. She has been showing my husband all of the important areas to rub. The first time around he sat in the waiting room the whole time. He felt totally left out. So this time he's really into the whole labor-coach thing. I swear he reads the pregnancy books more than I do!" Jean laughed, relieved to get back on a typical family topic.

"That's awesome! My husband read exactly one page—the page where they tell you how to catch the baby in an emergency. He was worried about having the baby in the car because I was determined to labor at home as long as possible. In the end we made it, but barely. Not to admit that my husband was right about something..." she joked.

"Oh it's okay to admit they're right when you're with your girlfriends, just not where they might hear you!" They both laughed, waking Julien from his nap. He might have been only five months, but he clearly already had developed his instinct for knowing when his mom had sat down to chat. Without taking him out of the sling, Wynn adjusted him onto her boob. Jean was impressed. Even though Jean nursed both of her children, she had never been able to pull off the no-hands sling nursing. When Maverick was a baby she didn't even know about slings, and when Sienna was a baby she had so much trouble nursing it required complete focus. In the end, and despite hundreds of bowls of oatmeal and gallons of nursing mom's tea, Jean had to supplement nursing with formula bottles because her milk never came in enough to be Sienna's sole nutrition. Jean made a mental note to buy a sling.

"Ouch!" Wynn reacted to Julien's bite by pushing his face into her boob, temporarily suffocating him.

"Is that how you do it? I don't remember what I did with Maverick, and with Sienna, I guess I never got enough milk going for her to bite me over it." Jean cringed at the admission of nursing Sienna, really laying it all out to a woman she'd just met. She wasn't always so forthright with her gritty details, but recently she noticed that life worked better if she was just herself. Less likely to have a bunch of assholes hanging around. Also, part of her felt compelled to tell the truth, since the truth was out there with a capital T barreling across the country right this very moment. Jean's stomach tensed at the thought of Maya, and a pang of heartburn stabbed at her chest. She reached for the economy-sized plastic bottle of Tums in her purse (despite the fact that her midwife recommended some all -natural plum paste, called umeboshi plum, that somehow never managed to get on the grocery list).

"You nursed your adopted daughter? I've never heard of that before. How did it work? Did your boobs just know what to do because you had already nursed your son?" Wynn asked, the restraint she showed earlier obviously overcome by curiosity. Jean didn't blame her. She crunched down on the chalky-sweet taste of the Tums and prepared to get into this delicate subject with a total stranger.

"It's getting more common. It's actually the sucking that causes the milk to come in, not the pregnancy. But I think it's way easier if you've already birthed a child, because there is something about pregnancy hormones that causes your milk ducts and alveoli to get bigger. I was also lucky, because I knew when I was getting the baby and I started pumping weeks beforehand. Stranger adoptions can be so uncertain..." Jean's voice trailed off at the look on Wynn's face, "Did I totally weird you out? I'm always afraid that people will be grossed out by Grandma nursing baby, even if they think that nursing is cool when it's an un-related adoption. It was just that Maverick and I had such a sweet nursing relationship, I couldn't bear the idea that Sienna wouldn't have the same thing. It was super hard, but I was such a breastfeeding purist back then, all judgmental about mom's who chose formula, which is totally ironic, because I ended up having to supplement with formula anyway."

"No! All of that sounds great to me," Wynn reassured Jean. "Sienna is lucky to have such a dedicated mother. Oh, and I totally get it about being a purist one moment and having that come back to bite you in the ass. It's the basic law of motherhood—the things you judge today will be your lot tomorrow!" Wynn said, wagging her finger at the air like she was giving instructions to an impertinent child.

"When Oliver was around one, I was in a play group with this two-year-old kid. He was constantly running around, throwing things, knocking babies over and being generally obnoxious. I was so annoyed that I actually stopped going to the group. Well, sure enough, when Oliver was two that same mom showed up at a playgroup with her new infant, and Oliver was being so rambunctious that she actually offered to lend me some book on raising a 'spirited child.' I was about to tell her that her older child may be 'spirited' or whatever the euphuism for ADD-brat is these days, but my darling Oliver was just exuberant. Except right then Oliver threw a toy car and actually hit her new baby's forehead!" Wynn laughed. She had a nice laugh, and her bright eyes crinkled easily along well-worn creases. Jean had always loved people with crinkly eyes; they give her a warm feeling. Santa Claus is always depicted with crinkly eyes. Jean noticed that her heartburn was gone.

"Oh, gawd, I hear that. Judging another child or mother is an instant curse on yourself," Jean agreed. "When Sienna was two, there were so many times when some other little kid threw a fit over nothing, and I secretly thanked myself for doing such a good job with Sienna—she hardly ever threw fits. But then she turned three, and do you know what she did this morning? She almost pushed her cereal bowl off the table because there were too many brown mini-wheats instead of white ones! I will do many things to please a child, but I draw the line at turning mini-wheats frost-side up."

Wynn laughed so hard her baby started crying, so they both got up and started walking toward Sienna and Oliver, who had wandered to the far side of the playground. Actually, what they were doing could only loosely be described as walking. Jean waddled like a 200-pound duck, and Wynn bounced along next to her like Tigger.

"Does Julien like that?" Jean asked a little incredulous. Rather than the little pat, pat, jiggle, jiggle Jean remembered doing with her babies, Wynn was jumping and swooping with her entire body. She whirled about with such gusto that she had to hold her baby so he didn't fly out of the sling and, frankly, if she hadn't held his head, Jean thought she might have to call child protective services to prevent shaken baby syndrome. It looked violent, but Julien wasn't crying anymore. The poor thing had stepped onto a roller coaster, and was probably so freaked he forgot to cry, Jean thought. She was about to say something when Wynn noticed the fear on her face and explained herself.

"Oliver had colic." Wynn nodded toward her older child as she bounded along. "He was one pissed-off baby. During the worst of it he screamed for seven or more hours a day. So I tried everything. We were going out of our minds. The standard sweet baby bouncing did nothing for him. Really, it just pissed him off even more. But I discovered if I really moved with my whole body, he calmed down. It was the same with noise. A simple 'shhh' from his mother's loving lips did nothing, but he could finally relax if I ran a vacuum next to his head. So I would strap him on and bounce around, vacuuming the entire house. And once I'd done the floors, walls, and ceilings of every room, and Oliver was finally sleeping peacefully, I'd sit down next to the running vacuum and cry."

"That sounds awful! I'm so lucky my babies didn't have colic. Does Julien?" Jean asked, with fear welling up inside about her new baby. People shouldn't tell pregnant women their baby nightmare stories. It was so easy to fall into the worry pit.

"No, thank God! But, he likes the full body bounce too. I think all babies like it. Just like a loud white noise, it distracts them from whatever discomfort they are suffering. I'm not big on baby experts, but the book on colic that suggested vigorous bouncing and running a vacuum saved my life."

"That's great. I didn't really know about books when I had Maverick; maybe there weren't as many available. But I read a ton when I got Sienna and, frankly, I don't think I found one piece of really useable advice. I just kept thinking that Sienna was so different than Maverick, how can any one 'baby expert' give advice applicable to all babies?"

"Oh, totally! It's like Oliver and Julien come from different planets. Forget men from Mars and women from Venus, I'm going with the astrologer's theory that everyone's got their own celestial configuration," Wynn agreed. Jean wondered if Wynn believed in astrology. Jean was completely unconvinced herself. Any theory that attracted so many flakes must be malarkey. But, when Marvin read this morning's paper, he announced that her horoscope said she would meet a new friend today.

"You know, I think that motherhood, or maybe just life in general, is trying to teach me that there is no point in forming opinions on anything. Opinions just turn and bite you in the ass later. After I got Sienna, I made a conscious decision to stop giving advice to other parents. So few of my hard-learned lessons with Maverick applied to her. Now when I talk with other moms, I try very hard to restrict my advice to 'this too shall pass' and 'don't be too hard on yourself'. I hate it when people give me advice, too. People are so full of themselves! They think they have the right answer for my child," Jean said, thinking of her mother's insistence that Maverick should be forced to finish his food when he was young. Thankfully she backed off by the time Jean had Sienna. But when Maverick was young her mother was still accustomed to treating Jean like a child. Jean *was* still a child.

"The moms with only one child are the worst, aren't they?" Wynn said with a conspiratorial giggle. Jean felt that little thrill women always feel when they're using righteous indignation, a time-honored glue, to cement their friendship together, even though just two seconds ago Jean had spouted off about her decision not to be judgmental. It was a deeply set addiction. "But you have to forgive them, right? Like you said, we were all happy advice givers at one point. I know I was. After you've clawed your way out of some snake-pit in child rearing, it's natural to want to reach back in and help another mom out."

Jean was about to tell her that she was right, they were addicted to judging like alcoholics were addicted to alcohol, they'd never be free of it, the best they could do was recognize the addiction and attempt a daily struggle against it. But Sienna's high-pitched scream distracted her. She had been looking at Wynn, and now realized that she couldn't see Sienna. Sienna was on the swing only a moment ago, airplane style, with her belly on the seat, arms and legs flying in the air. But where was she now? "Do you see Sienna?" Jean asked Wynn, turning in the direction the scream came from. What if someone grabbed her? Jean had been trying to teach Sienna about stranger danger, but the lesson wasn't going well. Yesterday Sienna ran half a block ahead of Jean when they were walking down the sidewalk and started up a conversation with an elderly couple. When Jean waddled up a good thirty seconds later Sienna announced loudly, "See, Mom? These strangers didn't grab me." The couple looked confused, and for once Jean was grateful that Sienna's lingering baby accent made it difficult for other people to understand her. Sienna screamed again, and this time Jean spotted her under the slide in a semi-enclosed area that was supposed to feel like a playhouse. The world has rarely seen a pregnant woman move so fast.

"What's wrong, sweetie?" Jean said, after managing to squat down low enough to poke her head through the "window," her concern for her daughter outweighing the fact that there was no hope of getting up again without help.

"He pushed me!" Sienna sobbed, pointing at Oliver.

"It was my turn to drive the truck!" Oliver defended, lunging his body toward a plastic steering wheel attached to the wall. Sienna blocked Oliver's attempt with her body and screamed again. This time, rather than panic, her wail caused Jean to feel annoyed. Was she really screaming like that over a steering wheel? They had been to this playground over a hundred times, and Jean had never seen Sienna express even the slightest interest before.

What is it about human nature that causes people

to want what others want? Why can't we just accept that we are hardwired to love different things so that we can have a multifaceted society?

A couple nights before, Sienna had asked Jean if she could sleep with her new shoes, because she loved them so much. It was sweet, but odd, because Sienna couldn't care less about clothes. So Jean asked her why. Sienna reported that Cindy at school said she loves shoes so much she sleeps with them. Cindy had the elite credentials of being a half-year older than Sienna and, as Jean had been made to understand, was therefore a direct conduit of God's law.

Jean tried to explain that some people have to love shoes so that we can have shoemakers. Other people have to love swings so we can have swing makers. If everyone loved the same thing, we wouldn't have all the different stuff we need. Jean had congratulated herself on a fabulous explanation. Not only did it fit the moment precisely, but it would tie in beautifully with a larger life lesson about following one's heart. Sienna gave her a worried look and tucked her new shoes under the covers.

"That's too loud, Sienna!" Jean said, covering her ears against the onslaught of the high-pitched lament. "You're hurting Mommy's ears."

"I'm the truck driver!" Sienna insisted, holding her ground against Oliver's pushing. Actually what she said was 'I the twuck dwiver," but it was clear that what she meant was 'back off, kid, this is *my* toy.'

"How about you both sing the ABC's, and when the song is over it will be Oliver's turn?" Wynn interjected. Jean hadn't heard this before, but it sounded brilliant. And it was: both kids started singing right away, displaying the self-assured pride of American children accustomed to being complimented for everything they do. No stranger to child ego-pumping, Jean recently posted a video of Sienna singing the song on YouTube, which she had entitled: "Elmo P" as in ...h, i, j, k, Elmo P... Sienna and Oliver took turns like that happily for about four rounds, and then Wynn gave Oliver a five-minute warning that they had to leave soon. Jean was more bummed than Oliver was.

"I'm going to ride my scooter home!" Oliver said, and took off running toward the place he had crashed it when they'd first arrived.

"Oh! Well, I guess he only needed a five-second warning. It was nice talking to you Jean," Wynn said, and started to walk away.

"Wait! Let me get your number. I'd love to get coffee with you sometime," Jean said. She had just been telling herself that she needed to rebuild a support network of friends now that she was starting over again with a new baby. She used to hang out with other moms a lot, but once she put Sienna in daycare and started working full time she had fallen out of the loop, except for the occasional prenatal yoga. Anyway, Wynn was way too cool to just let walk away.

"Oh! Great idea. Here, tell me your number and I'll call you," she said, unzipping a little pocket on the portion of her sling that hung down from the top of her shoulder. Her phone was covered in some crazy industrial-looking case.

"Wow, that looks like it could withstand a trip down the Amazon River," Jean said, giving her the number as Wynn helped Jean back up to standing.

"I know. I bought the toughest one I could find. Oliver likes to play with it, and I can't risk him breaking it. We can't afford another phone right now. Oh! Oliver, wait for me!" Oliver had scooted off the playground and was already on the sidewalk. Just then Julien woke up and let out a wail of his own. "Ack! Everything at once. I'd better go. I'll call you!" she yelled over her shoulder, and bounded off in a faster version of the crazy Tigger bounce-walk she had been doing before. The sight caused Jean to laugh. Not *at* Wynn, but with her, with all mothers, because motherhood can make you absolutely ridiculous. Because life can be so ridiculous. Because despite Jean's attitude about skinny moms and wackos who believe in astrology, she had a new friend. A good one.

CHAPTER FIVE

THAT FIRST NIGHT at the bar, Jesse had left Maya for a minute to go get more drinks, vanilla vodka and Coke for her and a gin and tonic for himself. Walking back towards her with the drinks in his hand he saw that the vultures had descended quickly. A slick fellow with a gold chain and a fake Gucci shirt leaned over and said something that caused her to laugh. Obviously, Jesse wasn't the only one trying to bag a fag hag. He edged closer, but the dude was blocking his path.

"I could tell from across the room that you would break my heart. Where will we meet after closing time?" Mr. Faux Gucci asked, as if it was a done deal.

Maya was quick and brutal. "We will meet in your dreams, sweetheart."

While slick-guy stood there with his mouth gaping, Jesse took the opportunity to push past with the drinks. "Wow, can't leave a woman alone here for ten minutes, huh?"

"Yep, I'm just a fawn in the jungle." She laughed before leading Jesse back to the thick of the dance floor. If she wasn't so fucking sexy, he would have been too intimidated to talk to her.

Jesse couldn't see past the end of his penis that night, but now he knew that Maya was no fawn. After this summer she had one more year to go before she graduated with a BA in Political Science, and she'd canceled a summer internship at some prestigious environmental organization to take this trip with him. He couldn't help but feel pale next to her. Maya was different from anyone he had ever met. She was originally from Northern California, which Jesse had always thought of as an exotic land filled with people just like him. For years he'd had elaborate fantasies about a mythical city called San Francisco, where the counterculture was so entrenched the mainstream flowed around it. He had planned at least ten road trips with friends to go there. (All of which fell flat due to fear of the unknown hiding behind "important" calendar items or lack of cash.)

She had also lived in Hawaii and Peru. All

through high school Jesse kept thinking that he was going to travel when he graduated. Instead of being some college goon, he was going to hitchhike across the United States and Mexico. Maybe Europe, too. He imagined himself bumping along late into the night in the back of some dusty farm truck, composing poetry that would become a bestseller after he died a lonely but romantic death. But then he got the job at the restaurant, and two years passed by in a flash. If he hadn't met Maya, he'd probably have put off his big adventure for years, if he ever went.

But he did meet her and now it was finally happening! Jesse was on his way to the Wild West and nothing could stop him now. Jesse savored the thought, half terror, that he may never return home, or if he does return, he will return a different man, perhaps a wiser man, weathered from the road, smelling like a mix of God's soil and exotic spices. He looked at the blur of suburbs out the window of the Greyhound bus. You could tell which developments were fancier by the height of the wall alongside the highway. He adjusted the little air vent above his head to blow right on his face and leaned back in his pleather seat. So many homes swishing by, each with their own family inside. So many lives with all of their stories, their love, their pain, encapsulated neatly into a house that took only a moment to pass by his window, half ignored and immediately forgotten. Jesse loved it. Goodbye suburbs! Goodbye lawns and goodbye fences!

Goodbye simple people content with simple lives. The grand adventure has begun. Anything could happen!

Jesse could feel the energy of the bus' large engine propelling them forward, faster and faster. But how fast were they really going? Traveling west was going against the rotation of the Earth so, perhaps, he wasn't really moving at all, relative to the sun. Jesse had seen a video on the internet that attempted to show the sun's movement through the cosmos, which as it turns out, is thousands of miles per hour causing the planets' path around the sun to look more like spirals than circles. The sun was moving, the Earth was moving and now, finally, Jesse was moving. All was right in the universe.

He went to squeeze Maya's hand, but she was taping away at her phone. So he leaned over and kissed her cheek. She looked up and smiled at him. He couldn't believe his luck: a beautiful woman, the adventure of a lifetime.

Their plan was to take buses a little past Pittsburg, just to get out of dodge as fast as possible, and then put their thumbs to the wind and feel the open road. The bus ride to Pittsburg was fairly smooth, just one big stopover in Baltimore, but when they arrived at the station they found out that the bus to Wheeling, West Virginia was running almost two hours behind.

Maya went to talk to the customer service people to make sure they had a seat while Jesse foraged for their lunch from a row of vending machines. They sat on the hard, plastic seats and whispered about the other travelers: Who was cheating on their spouse, who was meeting a long lost lover, who desperately needed to be arrested by the fashion police. After an hour the loud speaker announced that their bus was now three hours behind schedule. A very large woman in very tight acid washed jeans started yelling and swearing at customer service. Apparently she had a funeral to go to and if the fucking Greyhound agents would just get their fucking shit together and schedule things correctly she could still make it. Jesse started to feel really tired. They had had to get up at what Slaven liked to call "the ass crack of dawn" to catch the bus in D.C. and now they wouldn't get into Wheeling until late.

By the time they were on their way again, this time on a funkier regional bus, the glow of travel was already losing a bit of its luster. Maya had bought a copy of the Economist and was knee deep in some global financial crisis so Jesse tried to sleep. Unfortunately, the bus was packed with college students returning home for the summer who were excited to set their freedom off right with a little pre-partying. Jesse had a caffeinated soda in his backpack from the station so he drank it and started chatting with the kids around their seats.

Hunter and Brianna, sitting in front of them, were students at the Community College of Allegheny. They explained that the College had agreements with a few different universities so they were guaranteed admission to a four-year if they did well.

When Hunter found out Jesse was from Virginia he talked about a camping trip he was going on in Shenandoah National Park. Shenandoah was near where Jesse grew up and he'd been there several times with his Boy Scout troop. Plus, his mom drove Jesse and his sister along Skyline Drive every fall when the leaves started to turn.

Skyline drive runs along the crest of the Blue Ridge Mountains for over a hundred miles. Along every curve and turn you are treated to huge stunning views of the Shenandoah Valley to the west or the rolling Piedmont to the east. The park sets the speed limit low and purposefully leaves the roadsides unmowed so wildflowers crowd into the scenery and give the entire drive a lazy, happy feeling. In the fall the reds, oranges and purples are more magnificent than any Fourth of July fireworks display.

When they arrived in Wheeling, exhausted, Hunter asked his parents to give Jesse and Maya a ride to a motel out on the highway. They would rest up and start their grand hitchhiking adventure when they were fresh the next day. After checking in to their room, a dismally sad space with stains on the floor that even a busy pattern couldn't hide, Jesse noticed that the roof access down the hall was unlocked.

They climbed out into the night air and found a space between the vents to cuddle up with the motel's comforters. Other than the motel, a Denny's and a gas station, the area was pretty isolated, and they could see a few stars. A large star just overhead begged to be designated with importance. Certainly it played a major role in some constellation, or several, from various cultures around the globe. Maybe it was the eye of a bear, or the point of a spear thrown by a hero to pierce an evil heart.

Jesse tried to orient himself. The sun had set in front of them as they drove west. If the highway was straight, the star was in the north. Maybe it was Polaris, the North Star that had led countless sailors home through the wilderness of the sea. Jesse squeezed his body close to Maya. She was like his ship. With her he'd set sail to new lands, to adventures on the high seas.

Maya squeezed back, and soon they were ignoring the cool spring air, removing each other's clothes, making love in the soft glow of the Denny's yellow sign, a trail of white headlights zipping by below them only to redshift like starlight, and then slowly disappear into the distance.

"Can you believe we are just tiny, tiny humans on a tiny, tiny planet floating around some unimportant star in a galaxy that floats the ether with untold millions of other galaxies?" Jesse asked, his naked body wrapped taco-style with Maya's in the dirty comforter, his bodily fluids settling into the fibers alongside the many that had come before. Not that Jesse cared about the cleanliness of the blanket. He was thinking about stars. He loved how small he felt when stargazing. "How is it possible that we even exist at all? Isn't it silly that we feel important?"

"Maybe we evolved to feel important because it's a good survival mechanism," Maya suggested, but Jesse disagreed.

"No, I think we are important. Maybe we don't know why yet, maybe we won't figure it out in my lifetime, but humans are important. We were meant for something. That's why we are so superior to animals. We have some sort of destiny. There isn't any other explanation that makes sense."

Maya sat up, her white shoulders glowing against the night-black of her hair, which fell in a tangle down her back. It was so thick that if she leaned over Jesse and kissed him, her hair blocked out all light. Jesse was starting to think of the effect as the closing of a velvet bedroom curtain. "If we have a destiny, it seems like it must be to kill ourselves with a nuclear bomb or global warming," Maya said. "And I'm not so sure we are superior to animals. I saw a documentary on dolphins—you know they have a whole language and individual names?"

The ridiculousness of this comment shook Jesse out of his post-coital, stargazing reverie. "Oh, come on! Just look around. You can't seriously say that other animals are equal to humans. Dolphins may be whooping it up with names, but *we* are doing astrophysics. We build cities. We fly in the air and dive under water. And there has to be a reason for that. We can't just be doing all of these amazing things on this microscopic outpost in the cosmos for no reason."

Maya turned to look Jesse in the face. Her blue

eyes hit his brown ones with obvious surprise. Down on the highway there was a sudden screech of tires as a car merging onto the highway cut off another traveler. The car with the right of way honked loudly at the new intruder. "So, you believe in God?" Maya asked.

"I don't know." Jesse thought of his mom. She wasn't one of those born-again evangelists or anything, but she did love Jesus. They had always gone to the Reston Community Church for holiday services, and Sundays, too, when he and his sister were little. And she was big into prayer. Where he grew up, God wasn't something you believe in or don't believe in, God was simply part of the background noise of childhood, like manners and homework. "When I was a kid, Mom made us get on our knees and thank Jesus every night before bedtime. Sometimes I still do it. It helps clear my head, to come up with a list of things I'm grateful for at night. But I guess if I really think about it, I'm sure Jesus and God aren't real, at least not the way they talk about it in church, not beings that talk and think like humans. Not white guys with flowing robes listening to prayers and making judgments. It's more like they are a metaphor for something important, something big out there, some reason for our existence. An explanation for why humans are special. I believe in that."

"I've never been religious. Opiate of the masses," Maya said dismissively. "I can see how it might be nice to count your blessings every night, but religion has caused a lot more pain than good in the world. Just think of all of the wars between people over who was right about God." Maya leaned over to grab her shirt and jeans as she spoke. When she picked them up, a few pieces of the white gravel that covered the roof stuck to her clothing, and she had to stand up naked to shake them out. Her nipples tightened and her skin glowed in the light, but soon she was dressed. Jesse still held onto the warmth of the comforter, and the moment before the conversation switched from dreamy to what was starting to feel like an uncomfortable attack on his mother's way of life.

"Our church wasn't like that. Our pastor used to say that all of the different religions were fingers pointing at the same moon. The trick is to look at the moon and not fight about the fingers," Jesse said. He had liked that pastor, and the image of different people in their various religious garb standing around the planet with their fingers pointing out at one glorious moon.

"But that is just the thing, isn't it?" said Maya. "The moon is just a rock. It doesn't even have its own light. People think it's this big, mysterious thing, but really it's nothing. A small, inconsequential lump of stone in a huge universe. Looking at the fingers, looking at the moon. Both of them are a waste of time at best. A distraction from the reality. We should be looking at each other. Trying to figure out how to be kinder to each other, and how to live on this planet harmoniously with nature before we all fry from climate change."

Jesse stood up and shook out his own clothes, remembering to turn slightly so Maya wouldn't notice how small his penis looked in the cold air. "You sound so pessimistic. Humans have traveled to space. Don't you think that we'll figure out how to live on this planet without killing it? Or maybe make a new life somewhere up there?" Jesse waved his hand toward the stars. He'd much rather be talking about space travel. Someday humans will live in giant space stations, or maybe find another planet to inhabit.

"I don't think there is anything out there for us, Jesse. At least not where we can get at it. Did you know that they ended up having to pump extra oxygen into that closed-off biosphere in Arizona? The reason why we can't create a successful closed biosphere here on Earth is because we don't really understand the biosphere called Earth that we are living in. I don't think that's pessimistic. I just think that if we keep dreaming about God, or technology, or something else that will swoop in and save us, we'll never do the hard work to save ourselves. I'm actually an optimist. I think we can do it, but it isn't easy, and we have to stay focused."

Maya picked up the abandoned comforter and shook it out. Jesse used his hand to wipe off a few persistent bits, then helped her fold it. Once it was neatly squared, he took it from her hands so she wouldn't be burdened on the climb down. Jesse was, despite the nose piercing and black leather, still a

Southern boy. But instead of opening the door to the stairwell, he set the blanket back down and took both of Maya's hands.

"I agree with you that we should do what we have to do to keep our planet habitable, Maya, but there *is* something great around the corner for humans, I know it. Something big. And if we just have our worker bee hats on, recycling our cans, driving our hybrid cars, we could miss it. The real point of our existence isn't about just Earth." Jesse squeezed Maya's hands and gazed up. Maya looked tickled by his earnestness. She smiled, then leaned toward him and said, "Kiss me, dreamy," which may not have been a compliment, but Jesse kissed her anyway.

The next day they made the mistake of lounging around until checkout, having sex, and then taking turns in the small bathtub/shower stall before wandering over to the Denny's across the parking lot for breakfast. Jesse went first, and then watched the news while Maya took a long shower. It must take work to wash that hair. While she was in there, the entire room flooded with the amazing floral scent of some bathing product she must have brought with her, briefly turning the dingy hotel room into a spa-like oasis of scent.

On the news, the anchor was discussing the latest attempt to pass a bill on finance reform. Her black dress had a large vertical blue stripe down the front, giving the effect of a narrower physique than the one she had. Everything else about her was perfect though; perfect white teeth, perfect ebony complexion, perfectly straight hair. She was meant to slip past your notice, nothing to offend your senses and distract you from the news of the day. Jesse listened briefly to the finance debate, and then flipped it off. He'd heard it before. He lived in DC, after all, and frankly, he didn't see any of it mattering. As far as Jesse could tell they were all a bunch of corrupt fuckers that would do what they do regardless of this little reform or that minor twist. There wasn't any point in getting into a knot about it. Jesse had never voted, and didn't really see the point.

Sitting in the gold plastic booth at Denny's, Jesse looked over the colorful menu, each dish photographed in the best light, each calling, "Me! Pick me!" Jesse debated between the Philly Cheesesteak Omelet, which was what he usually ordered, and the Lumberjack Slam, because it was good to try something different. In the end he went with his usual, though. There was enough new going on in his life at the moment, he reasoned. And what if Denny's was an East Coast thing? What if this was his last Denny's? He asked Maya, but she just rolled her eyes and laughed. "They call this type of pit stop 'Anywhere America' because it is everywhere. Maybe not like McDonald's, but don't worry about it—you'll be able to find Denny's special brand of hormone-flushed, toxic crap food wherever you choose to travel in this great nation of ours." Then she ordered pancakes, probably hoping that it was the lesser evil. Jesse didn't comment when she ate the bacon that came with it.

CHAPTER SIX

THEY DIDN'T GET started hitching until after 1:00 p.m. By late afternoon the thrill was wearing thin. They got one ride pretty quickly, but it turned out to be a mistake, because the guy dropped them off on some little exit without any services or much traffic. Plus, the interstate overpassed the road, so the place where they had to wait, the beginning of the onramp, was too low to be visible to the people speeding by. Soon it was after five, and they were stuck. When hitchhiking you need a spot where people can see you a ways off; 15 seconds is perfect. They need to have time to suss you out and still have space to pull over. Ideally, there is another ten seconds or so of space after you in case they feel guilty about passing and change their mind. Jesse and Maya had maybe a total of five seconds at the bottom of the ramp, and most of those were due to a stop sign to their left, so not every car was turning onto the highway. Jesse knew that for most hitchhikers, the best call in this situation was to give up and start looking for a hidden spot to camp before it gets too dark; but most hitchhikers don't have his secret weapon. He had the one thing that every hitchhiker wishes they had, because it almost always guaranteed a ride: he had a woman.

They could hear the baby crying even before the driver rolled down her window. "I shouldn't pick up hitchhikers, but you two look sane enough. Where are you headed?" By 'sane' she meant 'harmless' because one of them was female. The difference between hitching with a woman and hitching alone is so dramatic that anyone studying sociology, or the differences between the sexes, should be forced to try it. If that many more people trust and care for females, then the males of our species must have something seriously wrong with them. Not that most men aren't sweet, honest, pussycats like Jesse, but way out there on the planes of the bell curve chart there must be more male psychos than female psychos. If you want to get anywhere fast in the hitchhiking world, you need to convince a woman to travel with you.

"We're going to Denver, so as far west as you will

take us, please." A warm wave of melting tension flooded Jesse's body. Maya had started to worry too, he could tell by the way she threw her backpack over only one shoulder and hurried to the car. Usually her movements were so precise, so elegant. But it was hard to be elegant while begging, and right now this Subaru was the only thing between them and camping on the side of the road.

"Well, I have to pull a long one tonight—just a bit past Bloomington, Illinois. So maybe we're all in luck. I could use someone to sit in the back and cheer up the baby." The wails from the back were miserable. Jesse looked at Maya; she was a woman, after all, even a mother technically. He indicated to Maya to take the back seat. She opened the door, but stood there for a moment, hesitating. Jesse could tell that she seriously doubted her ability to calm what sounded like a howling monster.

"Hi, I'm Jesse and that's Maya," Jesse said, climbing in the front seat before Maya could change her mind.

"Welcome to the witching hour Jesse and Maya. I'm Jada and the screamer in the back is Kayne," Jada said warmly.

"Would it help to just pull her out and feed her or something?" Maya asked, her voice raised to combat the noise. She still had not entered the car.

"The reason why I'm on this ramp is because I just tried that. Anyway, that is a tired cry, not a hungry cry," Jada said, her voice already changing from warm to annoyed. Maya was just standing there like a deer in the headlights letting cold air into the car. Jada probably regretted stopping. Jesse turned and tried to give Maya a meaningful look. A screaming baby was way better than camping on the side of the highway.

"Sorry, I don't know anything about babies. Um, wow, you must have a great mother instinct! I had no idea it was possible to tell the difference between cries." Maya exclaimed, obviously getting it and hoping the compliment caused the woman to forget her hesitation. Then she quickly climbed in next to the little fiend and buckled her seatbelt. Jesse buckled his seatbelt too. They were in.

"Ha! It is possible, and it's not instinct. No, I had to learn this stuff. If you look at his wide-open mouth and listen to the yowling tone of the crying — that is a tired cry. A hungry cry is created by a sucking motion in the mouth, it sounds more precise," she explained, and then after another shriek from the backseat she said, "It helps to sing to him. How about a round of 'Twinkle, Twinkle'?"

"Twinkle, Twinkle" surfaced from some deep, dusty corner of Jesse's brain and they sang. For the next twenty minutes they dug into their collective American consciences and sang every song they could think of, from the ABC's to "Yellow Submarine."

After the baby fell asleep, Maya said the singing reminded her of one time when she was in Mexico with her parents, and they had just hitched a ride in the back of someone's truck to check out a beach town that was off the bus routes. Her mother wanted to find migrating whales. When they arrived in Playa Azul it was empty, except for a few other international travelers sleeping on the beach in front of seasonally abandoned grass shacks that served as restaurants for vacationers from Mexico City during the holidays. A couple from Switzerland, some Canadians, a hot guy from New Zealand who was already traveling with an even hotter girl from Italy, an Israeli surfer, and thirteen-year-old Maya with her funky hippy parents. They were all standing around in a circle swapping travel stories and the latest on the dangers of the Mexico-Guatemala border when someone suddenly said, "Hey, everyone, let's do the hokey pokey!" And everyone knew it.

Jesse was completely turned on by the story. He wanted to be on that beach experiencing the commonalities of Western civilizations across the globe. He reached back through the space between the car wall and his seat to squeeze Maya's leg. Maya, his lifeboat, his pirate ship upon which he would sail the high seas and taste the treasures of the world. Then Maya adjusted her leg so that Jesse couldn't reach it anymore. A shock went through his body. Maybe he had misread her. Maybe she didn't want to be his lifeboat. Maybe, he comforted himself, he didn't need a lifeboat. Was he in danger of drowning? Honestly, deep inside, he knew that part of him had first grabbed onto her in order to save himself from the men in the club. Hot, sweaty, and purposefully trying to undermine Jesse's sexuality. Then he thought she would save him from the banality of being just another bartender in a city full of bartenders. Help him attain something truly exciting to set his life apart. But what was really going on between them? Were they really sailing off to exotic shores on an adventure of love? Why had she moved her leg away?

Jesse watched a blur of white and green turned into a legible highway sign. He wondered if he were driving whether he would have been able to read the sign in time to exit. He had a pair of glasses stashed in his backpack, but he also had a fantasy that his eyes would just improve on their own, without the crutch of glasses. At his last optometrist visit, which admittedly was several years ago when his mom was still making him appointments, his vision was 20/25. That is pretty close to 20/20, but not close enough. He bought a pair of dark-rimmed glasses from the sales section of the office and, for a couple days after, he considered changing his look from hipster punk to hipster geek, but his heart wasn't in it. So, he'd been doing eye strengthening exercises, forcing himself to look long distances and (trying to) remember to eat carrots.

It was not that glasses were bad, other than their basic inconvenience. Jesse actually thought they provided him with an incredible mind-opening experience. When he put the glasses on the world stayed as it was, but his eyes saw the world as changed. Except it hadn't changed, only his vision had improved.

The first day he got his glasses, he went around all day lifting them to see the world as he had known it, and lowering them to see the world as it had always been. He was so struck by how different the real world was that it forced him to consider whether there were other things in his life that he was seeing incorrectly due to lack of vision. What else had he misjudged due to the flaws in his own perception? He imagined that his glasses helped him to see the hard reality of life, the sharp edges and bright colors. This metaphorical use of glasses tickled the poet in him. Plus, it was a good conversation to have with buddies when stoned. Jesse and Slaven had talked about finding glasses that would allow them to expand their consciousness – to see the patterns on petals.

Jesse thought about the drugs he'd used to expand his consciousness. When he took MDMA, the pure stuff, the world appears to be a more beautiful, happy, peaceful, loving place than he normally perceived it to be. On a good dose, even wars seem an unhappy blip in a sea of kindness between all mankind. Drugs are like glasses. Or, his mother would probably argue, that they are the opposite of glasses, because they make you see the world as it is not. But which was the truth? Was war the inevitable outcome of man's basically greedy and jealous nature, or simply an eddy in the river of love? And more importantly, could he trust his own perception to tell him the truth of the matter either way? Jesse looked back at Maya, who was busy reading something on her phone. What about his perception of her? If he put the glasses on, would all the fuzzy sweetness he was feeling crisp up and leave him with someone he hardly knew, and probably had nothing in common with?

Jesse was so engrossed in this jumble that it took him an embarrassingly long time before he noticed that Jada was repeating over and over again, "Peanut butter, peanut butter, peanut butter..."

"I'm sorry, I guess I was spaced out," he apologized. This wasn't the first time that someone had used the peanut butter trick to make the point that Jesse was a crappy listener.

"That's okay, honey." She laughed. "I should be used to it. I have to repeat everything three times before my teenager responds. I asked if you two have a place to stay in Bloomington."

"My uncle lives in Denver, so we were planning on finding a motel near the highway tonight and hitching again tomorrow. You can drop us off anywhere that looks decent...but not too expensive," he added. For a split-second a lightning flash lit up the highway in front of them and a crackle of thunder shook the sky. Thank goodness they had found a ride.

"So you have a teen and a baby?" Jesse asked, to make up for rudely ignoring her, but also because he was honestly interested. Jesse's curiosity about people was as insatiable as a robot he saw in an old movie who came to life and went around saying

"More input! More input!"

"Well, my daughter is my husband's by birth, but, you know, I hate the term 'step-child', it sounds as if she isn't really mine," Jada replied.

Maya leaned forward and whispered, "Did you raise her from a baby?" Clearly Maya wanted to avoid waking the baby next to her. Jesse realized that little Kayne was probably about the same age Sienna was when Maya last saw her – another screaming baby.

"Not quite. She was almost three when I met Darren. Just the sweetest, prettiest little thing you've ever seen. Darren's a great man and all, but I'm not sure I would have been so quick to the altar if Melissa weren't part of the deal." Jada's brown eyes sparkled as she spoke with obvious affection.

"Do you get along with Melissa's, um, biological mother?" Jesse asked, starting to feel like he was stuck in a theme. Doesn't anyone have a normal, nuclear family anymore?

"Ha! 'Biological mother.' You college kids crack me up!" She laughed, and Jesse didn't correct her. Maya was the only 'college kid,' but he knew she was really referring to a particular socio-economic status and, despite the past two years of grungy city living, he guessed he still fit the category. "Her mom's all right when she isn't drinking. We visit her when AA has a strong hold, and avoid her when she falls off the wagon. When Melissa was a little kid we always tried to downplay the exact reason why Mommy Judy was unavailable, and during the tween years Melissa used to throw it in my face that I wasn't her 'real' mom, as if Judy would be sweeping in at any moment on a white chariot to save her from having to clean her room." Jada's joking tone did nothing to cover up that these scenes were obviously painful for her at the time. "Melissa's old enough now to have a better idea of what's really going on with her mom," she added.

"My best friend's dad is an alcoholic, and once he went sober he never looked back," Jesse offered. There was always hope. And, thinking of hope, Jesse reached back his hand again seeking Maya's leg. Maybe her earlier shift away didn't mean anything. He caught the inside of her thigh and started stroking it just above the knee. If she would only scoot a little forward...

"Oh, he looked back all right. You kids just didn't know about it. He may have never touched the booze again, but you bet your ass he looked back every day things got tough, and half of the easy days, too. Alcoholism is a bitch, let me tell you. Those Muslims may be wrong on a whole number of things, but they're right on alcohol. We'd all be better off without it. Course you'd have to pry the Budweiser out of my husband's cold, dead hand." Jada laughed, and Jesse decided that he liked her. He liked people who laugh easily. It occurred to him that Maya, who had not scooted forward and who again adjusted her leg so it was out of reach, hadn't been laughing very much on their trip. She did have a witty, wry sense of humor, but mostly he was starting to notice that she was pretty serious.

"But isn't that the point? Prohibition didn't work because no matter how evil alcohol is, people still want it. They want it so badly that there is no way government can stop them. I think the failed alcohol prohibition is a really good example why all prohibitions on drugs should end. They just don't work," Maya said.

"Oh, child, but they do work. Do you know how many crazy drug addicts would be running around this country if we just sold heroin at the street corner pharmacy? The reason why governments don't do that is because it's a bad idea. People are just too weak," Jada argued.

Jesse slunk down in his seat. The rain had reached them, or they had driven into the rain and it splatted against the window in big, fat drops. He watched the wipers steady, relentless migration back and forth across the window shield. He didn't have much to add to a conversation on drug prohibition, other than that he'd spent one lovely night last September in the drunk tank down at the jail on D Street praying to God that they didn't give him a blood test and find out what he was really on. Of course he could bust out his thoughts on how ecstasy had changed his perception, and maybe they could debate whether this change was for the better, if not for the more accurate. Or he could even offer to pull out the tiny silver canister he kept in the secret pocket of his backpack, but Jada probably wanted to stick to theoretical drug use.

"In Europe they are decriminalizing all sorts of drugs because they recognize that there already are drug addicts running around, and dealers selling heroin on the street corner. And, if your friend was addicted, where would you rather her buy it? At the street corner pharmacy, or a dealer?" Maya obviously didn't share Jesse's conflict-averse nature. Even though she was too fresh in his life to be "his" girlfriend, he felt proud of her for making such rational sounding arguments for the benefit of drug lovers everywhere. He reached back between the seats one more time to see if he she had shifted so could reach her leg, she hadn't.

"I am sorry, but I am so sick of liberals telling me about how much better Europe is. The population of the United States is in the hundreds of millions, and the population of Holland is, what, ten million? Maybe 20? Also, we have so much diversity, we have a ton of people who barely even speak English. It really isn't fair to compare us to Europe" Jada was also quite willing to engage. It was no wonder the *Times* recently reported that the population of female law students was increasing so dramatically, Jesse thought. Women were definitely on their way to taking over. Maybe he should have sat in the back with the baby. "...And if my friend was on heroin, I would want to help her get *off* the drug, not get more of it," Jada finished.

"But the point is that she *would* want more of it, and she would find it, but where? It's the government's job to decide that. No matter how many people there are in a country. A decision to not sell it at the pharmacy is a decision to sell it on the street corner," Maya argued, her voice slipping above her formally careful whisper. Why was Maya arguing with Jada? Didn't she know that the woman could pull over at any moment and leave them in the storm? What is the point? Jesse turned to look at her and noticed her taught body was strained against the seatbelt. She looked like she was trying to physically escape the back seat through the space between the front seats. No wonder he couldn't reach her down the side. He looked at the sleeping baby, maybe it wasn't a good idea to have Maya sit next to him. She looked totally stressed.

"What about decriminalization? Isn't that a happy medium?" Jesse finally offered, to reduce the tension. "Don't make it widely and easily available, but don't throw the users in jail, either. Put them in clinics or something."

"I'm not paying for some drug addict to just lounge around and find themselves," Jada laughed.

"You pay for them anyway when they show up at the emergency room," Maya retorted. Jesse thought Jada would be offended, but she kept smiling.

"All right, smarties. If college students were in charge it would be free sex, drugs, and rock and roll for all." Jada laughed again. "You know, I think you should stay at my place tonight. Darren would get a kick out of having a couple college liberals around to banter with for a day. If you mow my lawn in the morning, I won't even charge you for breakfast."

CHAPTER SEVEN

THEY TURNED LEFT down a narrow street without sidewalks. From the light of one yellow streetlamp, Jesse could see that some neighbors weren't keeping up their lawn as fastidiously as others. His mother had always kept careful tabs on the neighborhood yards. She was the head of the neighborhood association's yard committee. Considering how seriously she took it, she might have invented the committee. Where she grew up, people were as likely to keep broken-down cars in their front yards as grass, so it was a point of pride to live in a neighborhood with rules that forced people to keep it neat. When Jesse was little, she would bring him along with her on Saturdays to hand out warning citations. She could have mailed them, but she said people just toss things that come in the mail. In order to get compliance without having to resort to nasty fines, it was best to approach a problem personally. It was her way of keeping the neighbors in line, keeping everyone friendly, and establishing her position as a person of authority.

Every once in a while, an immigrant would move into the community and attempt to put some sort of shaggy veggie garden in their front yard. Jesse's mom would go on high alert. She took pride in her Southern hospitality, so she would spend days plotting her approach to the renegades. When she felt she was prepared, she would drag Jesse (somehow Trish always got out of these things) and her small arsenal of phrase books in various languages. "Nín hǎo!" she would smile and greet the unsuspecting newcomers, before explaining that things were different here in America. There are rules, and fines... I'm sure you understand. She would have a big smile plastered on her face the whole time, but on the way home she would be on the telephone with her girlfriends, yapping away about how these awful people were taking over the country.

For most of his childhood, Jesse assumed that what his mother said about immigrants taking people's jobs was true, but once he started working in restaurants he realized that it is the immigrants that basically keep the country ticking with their cheap behind-the-scenes labor. They do the jobs nobody else wants. Jobs that need to be done.

One time he made the mistake of telling a Uruguayan girl his enlightened observations about immigrants. He even went as far as saying that the foreigners washing dishes were harder workers than the white guys at the front of the restaurant, and other self-depreciating compliments he thought she would appreciate. He also said, and the memory of it makes him cringe to think of it, that he planned on traveling "south" to get a feel for where his "friends" came from (this despite the fact that over the course of the two years he worked there he had never bothered to learn the names of most of the kitchen staff, other than José, who for some reason unknown to Jesse spoke English well). Instead of being wooed, the girl answered with disdain, "American kids backpack around South America, patting themselves for being so much more culturally conscious than the wealthy tour-bus tourists, but the fact is that you're all there to stare at the little brown people. We are all the same to you. You probably think I grew up eating burritos." That was the last time Jesse tried that line, but he did do a little research into Uruguayan food (which, as it turns out, is nothing like the stuff they serve at the Baja Rico taco bar).

As Jada turned into her driveway, the headlights traveled briefly over a camo-colored mailbox with what appeared to be fake antlers glued to the top.

The manufactured house looked gray in the night, but where the porch light shone you could see it was actually a dusty blue color. Jesse got out of the car and carefully stepped over a bicycle that was casually left on the ground. This relieved him. The neighborhood must be safe enough if the homeowners assumed it wouldn't be stolen. Maya was still asleep in back, and Jesse felt grateful that he could wake her and lead her just a few steps to a warm house instead of a long walk in the dark to find a motel room. He was also stoked to save the money. When Maya said she didn't have any money for the trip she was being honest. He'd had to pay for everything.

"Would you mind grabbing the suitcase out of the back so I can bring in the baby?" Jada whispered to Jesse, indicating that the baby would be easily wakened without the whirl of the car engine to ease his sleep. He waited until she delicately extracted the car seat from its perch and headed toward the house before he popped the hatchback and woke Maya. Jada had called ahead so the pull out sofa was already made up in the first room they entered. Jada quickly disappeared down a hall with the baby leaving Jesse and Maya the luxury of a clean, private bed.

The next morning Maya helped Jada with the dishes, while Jesse did the manly thing and slunk off to the living room, where Darren was already watching NASCAR. He had mowed the lawn earlier and Jada hadn't thought of anything else for him to do. Unfortunately, being almost completely devoid of athletic ability or interest, Jesse was one of the few males on the planet that couldn't just instantly buddy up with a stranger over the latest sports scores. He wasn't even sure if NASCAR was a sport. The only thing Jesse knew about NASCAR was that cars race in circles around a track. And that it was mostly a redneck thing. Jesse looked over at Darren. He had never met a black redneck before, so somewhere he'd miscalculated his assumptions (about black people or NASCAR or rednecks, Jesse couldn't tell you).

The living room was cozy and dark, with the TV providing most of the light. Jesse flopped down on the couch, which he had folded back into its proper position earlier. It was so covered with mismatched throw pillows and afghans it was actually hard to find a place to sit. The baby was crawling around on the floor and, when he came close, he grabbed Jesse's leg and attempted to pull himself to standing. Melissa, the teenager, was sitting on yet another pillow on the floor, painting her toenails a sparkly teal color. The fumes of the polish plus the smoke from Darren's Camel cigarette quickly combined to make a perfect migraine storm in Jesse's head.

Jesse was accustomed to smoke. Virginia and the District of Columbia are both populated with the greatest lovers of the cancer stick you will find. He even smoked a bit himself here and there. But everyone knows the shit kills babies, right? Jesse briefly pondered the ethical dilemma of nagging the husband of a woman who had literally taken him off the street and into a warm bed. He thought of the fire training he'd had in fourth grade. The fireman came to their school to teach the kids the all-important "stop, drop, and roll" technique. The fireman, whom he clearly remembered had muscles bulging out all over the place, had told them to always crawl in a smoky house, because for some reason there was less smoke within a foot of the floor. Jesse had firmly committed this crucial tip to memory despite the fact that it doesn't make sense at all, since presumably the particles in the smoke are heavy. Maybe it had something to do with heat rising; but if it is hot enough to force the smoke particles up higher in the air doesn't that mean that you are crawling on the fire?

Anyway, maybe this baby was safe, Jesse thought. Given his utter failure at utilizing Jesse's leg as leverage to climb to his feet (the baby had barely climbed three inches before plopping down on its fat diapered bottom), he was clearly incapable of rising into the danger zone. Maybe the crawling phase was God's way of helping caveman babies avoid campfire smoke during critical brain development. Plus, Jesse's mom told him that his dad used to smoke cigars. Not that a pierced, punk bartender was the dream plan that every mother had for her child, but Jesse thought he'd turned out all right.

Maya and Jada were cracking up in the kitchen. They'd had freezer waffles, maple flavored corn-syrup, and freezer sausage links for breakfast. Or at least most of them had that; the baby had a banana, and Jesse wasn't sure Jada ate anything because she never sat down. He gave up on NASCAR and walked into the kitchen to avoid the looming migraine. Just in time to hear Jada trying to sell her husband.

"Oh, come on, now, he's a good-looking fellow! You'd learn to love him," she joked.

"Wouldn't you feel jealous? Isn't that most women's nightmare: their husbands falling in love with the next new thing?" Maya asked.

"I don't know. Sometimes when I'm alone in the kitchen I call my girlfriend and joke that whoever made bigamy illegal was a misogynistic bastard trying to divide and conquer us." Jada's tone got serious with the accusation, but her eyes twinkled. She was obviously being sarcastic. "No woman should be stuck with cooking, cleaning, and babies without at least one or two other wives to help out," she added, and rinsed off the last of the breakfast dishes to load them into the dishwasher. Jesse reached into the sink and grabbed a sponge. The table still had syrup spills on it from the baby. Maya was tackling the baby seat, which was pretty gross. Jada had given the baby bits of waffles to try and, although it was possible that some of it actually got into his mouth, most of it just served its purpose as a five-second diversion and ended up in sticky crumbs all over the seat. And the floor. With this much of a mess after only one meal, it wasn't any wonder that she wanted a little help. What about Darren and

Melissa? Jesse and his sister had to clean up after meals when they were Melissa's age.

"But, what about the sex?" Maya half-whispered.

Jada laughed. "Oh, sweetie, those first years when your children are nursing, crying, or just pulling at you all day and half the night—more women than not would be just as happy if their hubbies would go tugging on some fresh blood and let them be. Not that I advocate turning them away. Fact is—and you should remember this—a marriage is just like a garden. It needs weeding, watering, and sun to produce results. Having sex when you're not in the mood is weeding, has to be done for the health of the garden, and pleasant enough once you get going. So many couples let the sex go by the wayside after they have children and it's a bad habit. The more sex you have, the more you'll want to have, and it works the other way, too—take my word on it, or you're headed for trouble."

"What happened to women's liberation, Jada?! First you say you want your man to have a harem, with all the women stuck home with babies, and then you tell me I have to sexually please my man even when I'm not in the mood? What century are you from? My feminist studies prof would have a field day with you!" Maya's voice was almost giddy. She was sparring. Jesse was starting to get the impression that she was happiest sparring.

"Jeez, girl, you know I'm just kidding, right? Of course, if you actually ever touched my husband I'd have to kill you! And anyway, I never said that all women have to be stuck in the house with babies. I'm one hundred percent for equal opportunity for women in the workforce—but let me tell you something. Something I bet your feminist studies prof forgot to mention in her tirades about fair pay: It doesn't matter what century or culture you're dealing with, all people have to adapt a civilization around a few basic facts: the women have the wombs, and the women have the boobs. I just read a book that says babies should breastfeed for at least a year. A year! Add that to a bed-rest pregnancy, and lame-ass breast pumps that don't work, and you could be out of the full-time workforce for almost two years *per kid*. Anyway, with the cost of childcare these days, a lot of my friends have stayed home because the tuition is higher than their salaries were. Like I said, ain't nobody going to touch my Darrel, but facts are facts: more wives are an economic solution to an age old problem. In a harem you could have the mothers that liked to be home, home, and the rest of the wives working. The ones at home could even nurse your kids for you, 'cause wet-nursing is another centuries-old traditional answer to the problem that mothering takes time and many women are needed elsewhere." Despite claiming that she was joking, Jada actually looked excited at this thought, maybe even a bit manic. Jesse wanted to point out that the teenager painting her toenails in the den could be helping more, but he didn't. Who knew what the deal was with that. Best not to get involved in people's households. Except then he had nothing to add. He scrubbed at a bit of dried jelly on the table.

"What about employers just making it easier to breastfeed at work? I swear I heard that employers have to provide a room or something. I saw a debate on C-SPAN" Maya said, obviously forgetting that nobody outside the Beltway watches C-SPAN. Living in DC had turned her into a political junkie. Jesse had seen it happen before. He made it almost a point of pride to keep out of that mud pit.

"Those laws are about making it easier to pump breast milk, not breastfeed. Do you have any idea how hard it is to get desk work done with an eight-month-old hanging on your boob? Sure, I can throw him in a backpack carrier to vacuum, or sway him to sleep while doing dishes, but sitting at a desk for eight hours? He'd scream his brains out!" Jada said.

Was she suggesting that mothers should be paid just to stay home with their babies? Jesse had heard his mom rant about how black welfare queens have it so easy, while hardworking, tax-paying people like her struggle. He had never been interested enough to consider whether or not any of it was true, but he'd been in the room for over ten minutes now without saying anything and this, at least, was something he had heard about.

"Well, what are the alternatives?" he argued, trying to make his tone sound as if he really cared. "We can't just have the government paying women to stay home and have babies. Welfare queens?" He looked around at the two woman. Surely they'd heard of welfare queens.

"Plus, any government program that encourages more than one baby is bad for the environment. Overpopulation of the planet and all that," Maya said. Jesse was encouraged. Maybe Maya felt like they were on the same team here. Not being on the same team, he was starting to realize, would probably be painful.

"The government *should* use tax money for maternity leave," said Jada, obviously worked up about this issue. "Okay, I can see that allowing someone to live on the dole for ten babies doesn't really make sense for the economy or the planet, but what about two? Most other industrial countries give a paid year off for the mom for each baby, and a few give more than that. Think of the additional benefit to an entire population if every person had a loving mother with them every day of their first year."

"Don't forget about loving daddies. We want a year off too!" Jesse joked. All of this woman-centered stuff was what generally annoyed him about feminism. And, anyway, someone needed to break the tension. Unless it was used in some ironic way to add comedy to a play, Jesse was generally bored and a little uncomfortable around politics. Although it gave people something to talk about, like sports, he felt that political discussions mostly miss the point of life, like a bunch of people hovered around a chessboard in DuPont Circle completely ignoring a gorgeous winter day.

"Grow a pair of boobs and we'll talk," Jada teased him right back. But instead of keeping the tone light, she got serious again. "Actually, I totally agree that dads should get a little paid time off from work to bond with their babies, too."

Maya, spotting a weakness, went in for the slam dunk. "But Jesse makes a good point; moms don't have to be the only one. What about pumping? That's adequate nutrition for babies, right?"

"Adequate nutrition? You sound like the Surgeon General! Sure, lots of moms pump—but for how long? It's an uncomfortable hassle, and plenty of babies have a hard time adjusting back and forth between the real and rubber tit. I'd like to see statistics on how many moms forced to pump actually make it to a year of breast milk. Anyway, one of the benefits of breastfeeding is that the mom's milk assists the baby's immune system by passing along mom's immune response to the baby. How is that going to work if the mom and baby are in different places, being exposed to different germs?" Jada was not backing down yet. This was obviously a sensitive topic, a life choice decision she was battling out on Judgment Fields.

Jesse dumped the crumbs he had wiped off the table into the trash and looked over at Maya. Her face looked pained and she was scrubbing a little too hard on some invisible stain on the highchair tray. Was it the breastfeeding thing? Jesse was feeling a little pained as well. He glanced at the doorway and considered whether to get back to NASCAR and toxic fumes before these women start debating the politics of their periods. Then it occurred to Jesse that Maya had a baby she'd never breastfed.

"Well, we're going to have to agree to disagree on this subject, Jada," Maya said, after a few seconds pause. Maybe she had debated whether or not to tell Jada about Sienna. "I'm all for natural breastfeeding and everything, but it isn't the end-all-be-all for babies. They need loving homes. You make it seem like adopted babies are screwed." The whine seeping into Maya's voice was interesting to watch. This was the first time Jesse had seen her lose her cool, even a touch. The subject must be too raw for her. His mother was always quipping that a mother's life was "guilt if you do, guilt if you don't." The look on Maya's face showed that the adoption hadn't spared her this fate.

Jada caught on to Maya's hurt, but didn't guess its source. "Oh, gosh, I didn't mean to offend you, Maya. Were you adopted? I'm sorry to come off all righteous. I know that these things are secondary to love—of course they are. I just get all flustered thinking that woman are so encouraged to put their babies second."

"Well, sometimes putting a baby first looks a lot like putting her second." Maya said quietly.

"Oh, I know, sweetie, I know," Jada said, and went over to hug Maya without asking for any more details. Jesse looked at these two women who had done nothing but find things to argue about since they first laid eyes on each other. It was like they were part of some magical woman's club where they argue until they are blue in the face, but when life kicks it all to smithereens, they brush it aside and hold each other up. He felt the sting of jealousy. He was reminded of his mother and sister, who fight like dogs, but also have a connection so deep even Jesse sat on its sidelines. Jesse always avoided fights because inside he felt that love, at least the love anyone felt for him, was too fragile.

CHAPTER EIGHT

SHE WANTS THE house, some stability for the kids," Jean's opposing counsel, Roy Perton said over the telephone line, already sounding exhausted. It was Friday at 4:40 in the afternoon and they were trying to hash out a settlement to avoid court on Monday.

"Oh, come on, Roy. They're middle class. You know she can't have the house," Jean replied. It's the first rule in family law: mom wants the house but she can't afford to keep the house. Spousal support doesn't cover the mortgage. Husband needs the equity to buy a condo, blah blah blah, it's the same story over and over again. In this case, Jean's client was a computer programmer, but not one of those hot shots. His salary barely covered their expenses, what with the expensive Santa Cruz mortgage and those four kids. But Roy had to go through the motions and ask, just like Jean did when she represented the wife. The law requires lawyers to be "zealous" advocates, and anyway, you get paid in six-minute increments for negotiating for what your client wants, even if it's futile.

"They have four children under ten years old. It's going to be impossible to find anything else in the school district with that measly spousal support he's offering."

"Roy! You have to tell her to stop this sniveling. She can't have the house. These people don't have enough money to drag this out in court. You were there this morning. John Blackwell had that mom who stayed home with her Down Syndrome child— the kid couldn't wipe his own ass, Roy—and Judge Patron ordered the house sold before we broke for lunch. When the entire value of the estate is buried in a house, you have to sell and divide, there's no way around it," Even though there is technically a law that allows Judges to postpone a sale, every lawyer in court that morning could have predicted the outcome before the hearing started. The mom didn't have a chance and Blackwell was just there to give his client her day in court and line his pocketbook. Certain angry clients would rather fight for the impossible than settle for the realistic and Blackwell specialized in that set. Jean preferred clients who wanted to get through the divorce process as smoothly and efficiently as possible, people who listened to counsel. Plus, she hated losing in court. Of course, family law lawyers get paid whether they win or lose. Many lawyers have put their children through college fighting for their clients' lost causes. It irked Jean though, felt like a conflict of interest. This was why Blackwell drove a Mercedes and Jean drove a Subaru.

"This case is different, Jean. They've got the beach house. He could live there—or take a mortgage against it until the children are older."

"The beach house was his inheritance, Roy. It's off limits, you know that." In California, inheritances are considered "separate property" and they don't get divided in a divorce. Jean's client, Tom Switzer, had inherited a one-bedroom beach house a little farther north on the coast from his grandparents. It was a beautiful place, worth almost two million dollars. His entire family, all wealthy, used it as a vacation getaway for free, but it did technically belong only to Tom and Roy was correct that the Judge would consider its potential as available housing when deciding on whether to grant a motion for a deferred sale.

"If we go to court on Monday, I'm bringing a stack of photographs from vacations. I've got the beach house, a condo in Vail they rented with Tom's mother last Christmas, and some family reunion in Hawaii a few years back. I'm arguing for an increase in spousal support based on lifestyle," Roy said, playing his best card. It was a decent argument. The equation for child support was mostly set, but the judge has a lot of leeway to adjust spousal support to fit the circumstances, the "marital standard of living," especially in situations like this where the couple enjoyed a higher standard of living than their W-2's indicated.

Jean had seen this one coming; she'd prepped her client. "Okay, Roy. It's getting late. Let's just finish this. We'll increase it by three hundred a month for two years. That's plenty of time to get the baby out of arms and into preschool. You have to tell her the facts: unless she's got a wealthy boyfriend waiting in the wings, she is going to have to start working at some point."

Jean expected Roy to ask for more. They'd been assigned to Judge Randall, not Judge Patron. Randall was known to go a little softer on women getting dumped, especially stay-at-home mothers. His wife had never worked, and from what Jean had seen at bar events, he treated her like a queen. But all Roy said was "What about the house?" reminding Jean of the fact that Roy still worked for her old bosses, the Hanson brothers, who hadn't offered anyone partnership in twenty years of business. Roy was a pushover.

"We'll wait until spring to sell the house; the market's better then, anyway. But that's it, Roy. It will be sold in the spring. I want her signature on that deal before court Monday, or the spousal support offer is off the table."

Jean felt exhilarated when she hung up. The high of the battle. Now she would be able to tell her client she had settled for three hundred, even though she had warned him the increase would be closer to five. Tom Switzer would be singing her praises all over town and hopefully on a few of those pesky review sites. In this day and age a good review could bring a flood of cash. Jean wanted to trade her Subaru in for one of those new minivans now that they were going to be a family of five. Minivans had officially gone from frumpy to hip and Jean needed a little extra cash to get in on the trend. Her neighbor recently bought one that was so tricked out the entire block had gathered to ooh and awe over it. The thing had a doublewide screen and a vacuum cleaner.

Of course, the time for earning this cash was getting as tight as the waistline of Jean's pants, but she didn't dwell on it long. Jean was deep in the rabbit hole of denial. Or, if not denial, then deer-in-the-headlights paralysis. She had no plan for care, she still hadn't interviewed a single nanny, but she just took another client earlier that day with only a casual mention that she won't be as available when the baby arrives. She couldn't bring herself to turn it away. It was a startup business, her favorite type of client. A young man with stars in his eyes, a little money from Grandpa, and a half-baked business plan to grow mushrooms in coffee bean husks. Jean loved helping the big dreamers massage and shape their fresh businesses like soft dough. Though, truthfully, she probably would have taken any sort of client. Jean was addicted to working.

Not that she had never been able to quit before. When Sienna was born, Jean intended to dedicate herself entirely to the baby. She left the Hanson firm, poured a chunk of their savings into upgrading and advertising the Divine Center, and prepared herself for a solid year of motherhood before she went back to law. Except the tedium of staying in the house with an infant day after day nearly killed her. She ended up starting her own law office when Sienna was a couple of months old. She started small, only had a few clients at first, Sienna often slept or played in her bassinet in the corner. But after a few months Jean had enough clients to necessitate hiring Shelia, a college student, as a part-time mommy's helper. Sheila would jog Sienna in that big Bob stroller over to the park when Jean had clients and then stroll her back for Mommy time. Then Sheila took off to follow a surfer down to Costa Rica and Jean enrolled Sienna in daycare.

Ever since Sienna started daycare at the darling age of 11 ½ months, Jean has spent a solid 50 hours a week at the office. Fifty hours a week doesn't qualify a lawyer for the workaholic title normally, most lawyers put in more hours than that, but most lawyers are not the mothers of young children. Mothers of young children, Jean had often chided herself, were supposed to keep to 40 hours a week or less, unless they were career-obsessed workaholics, cold-hearted enough to ignore their precious children. On days when she didn't even make it back home in time for Sienna's goodnight kiss, and the devil on her shoulder whispered into her ear that she was a terrible mother, she pointed to that first (almost) year as evidence that she was a good mother after all. A good mother that gave her daughter a solid start. An (almost) full year of Mommy's (mostly) undivided attention. Because her identity as a good mother depended on it, Jean intended to give baby Arvin a similar chunk of devoted time before diving back into work, at least a taste of the single-minded focus every child deserves. Except, it was obviously not going to happen. She didn't quite know how to press pause. And she didn't really want to.

This wasn't an issue with Maverick. After Maverick was born, Marvin and Jean accepted the fact that parenthood was their life; not a fancy university, not partying with their friends, but playing house with a cute baby boy. It could have been a day-time special or a cautionary tale for other teen parents, but it wasn't. They were actually pretty happy in that tiny apartment above the garage. Her parents didn't charge them rent. Marvin got his massage license and was funny and handsome enough to quickly attract a devoted following at an uptown spa. Jean finished up high school and started taking community college courses while her mother helped with Maverick. The college courses not only provided Jean with intellectual stimulation, they gave her access to scholarships, which enabled them to save up a little nest egg.

When Maverick was eight, Jean got a great scholarship to Lincoln Law School. Then Marvin got the opportunity to buy a friend's funky old yoga studio near Marvin's grandparent's home in Santa Cruz. Moving to the other side of the Santa Cruz Mountains meant Jean would have to deal with a treacherous commute back over the hill for the four-year law program in San Jose, but she agreed to the move.

Marvin's grandparents offered them a deep discount on a rental they owned and Marvin argued successfully that no one in their right mind would pass up an opportunity to raise their son in Santa Cruz. With its fresh sea air, world class surfing and mountain biking, and small coastal town feel Santa Cruz offered everything little Maverick could possibly want.

When she finished law school Jean applied to every firm in town and got an offer from the Hanson brothers to be their latest associate. Latest because associates didn't last very long at that firm, as Jean soon discovered. The brothers believed in hiring associates, throwing them into a trial by fire, and then leaving to play golf, which was either a great way to separate the cream from the milk or to get sued for malpractice. Unlike many before her, Jean had excelled in that harsh environment and it was an exciting time in her life. The Hanson firm was just around the corner from the courthouse on Ocean Street and she was in court almost every day.

Marvin had the flexibility to hang out with Maverick after school so Jean dove headlong into her career.

Then, Maverick's junior year of high school, Sienna happened. Marvin and Jean both knew instantly that they wanted the baby. They had been talking off and on for a long time about having another baby, but the timing just never seemed right. How could she plan to have a baby when she worked twelve-hour days at the firm? "Is there ever a right time to have a baby?" Jean's mother asked during one of their marathon telephone conversations. "Just take the IUD out and let God decide!" her dad had joked. Jean simply could not fathom the idea of choosing to leave her work. Leaving the clients who needed her. The beauty of Sienna coming into their life the way she did was that they didn't plan it. Just like Maverick before her, Sienna simply derailed the current life and knocked them into parenting. A real baby, with an arrival date, forces a person to make decisions. Jean had been tinkering around with the idea of starting her own firm someday, and realized that Sienna was the perfect excuse to make that career leap. She would take a year off to mother Sienna, and then find the perfect office space to start her own practice.

Things weren't so clear-cut with this baby. Now that she worked for herself, she couldn't neatly bookend a baby's first year between career moves. Although she had tried to reduce her caseload, only taking on clients who were aware of her pregnancy and the fact that she would be less available for a few months after the baby was born, she was still working full time. And "less" available, still meant available, she had assured her clients. Jean was afraid that if she completely fell of the map, even for a few months, she'd lose everything she worked for: her reputation, her client list, and the independence of working for herself.

On the other hand, like so many California women with means, Jean was determined to give her baby the best possible start in life, right in mommy's arms. At mommy's breast. Jean's image of her baby's first year did not include spending every daylight hour with a nanny who wasn't bonded by blood to love him. Rather than strategize a plan for this imminent reality, Jean was doing what she had been doing for the last nine months: trying her best to ignore it.

CHAPTER NINE

THEY ROLLED UP their mats, said their good-byes, and made a bee-line for the adjacent French bakery. As they dashed across the small courtyard (as fast as two pregnant women are capable of dashing), Kim and Jean joked that they only went to pre-natal yoga because it granted them the license to eat whatever they wanted at the bakery afterward. The truth was, though, that they liked the yoga class. There was nothing like getting together with other pregnant women to compare notes. Over the past eight months they'd shared tips on everything from the best pillow arrangement for sleeping, to choosing doctors, and they'd been a support for each other until, one by one, they'd been picked off by the birth of a baby. Unless someone jumped the gun, Jean was next.

Kim especially had been a good support for Jean. They'd been friendly when they worked at the same law firm years earlier, but not true friends. Frankly, Kim was intimidating. It wasn't just that she was classically beautiful, with wide-set eyes and long, straight blond hair; she was also gloriously stylish. It was unnerving back then, but when Kim turned up in yoga class, she acted so glad to bond with an "old friend" that Jean couldn't help but be glad back. Kim was only six months along, though, so they would be in different categories soon.

Part of Jean felt a little sad at the loss of her prenatal group, but she remembered from when Sienna was a baby that there would be more groups. Stroller walking groups that went along West Cliff, with waves crashing below, had been her favorite. She saw so many dolphins and sea otters when Sienna was a baby because, when your job was to walk your baby to sleep, you actually have time to look for them. Even though they live four short blocks from the ocean, Jean hadn't seen a pod of dolphins in years. After Sienna started daycare and her law firm took off, she ignored the promise she had made to herself to jog along the seaside, and instead joined a gym. The seaside was only open during daylight hours, and her schedule required more flexibility. You'd think they would be down there every weekend, shovel and pail in hand, building castles with walls high enough to battle the onslaught of waves. But, frankly, it was just easier to walk down the street to the playground than get everything together for the beach.

When Jean did get down to the beach, she spent the entire time chasing Sienna, petrified that she would wander too deep into the cold water and drown before Jean had a chance to grab her. For the most part, it was a ridiculous worry. The waves weren't treacherous there, and Sienna was a cautious girl. But once when Maverick was about eight, they had gone camping on a remote beach with a strong undertow and their old, blind dog got dragged in. When Jean realized what was happening she was in a panic over the dog, but even more scared that Maverick, standing almost twenty feet away from her, closer to the ocean than he was to her, was going to jump in before Jean could reach him. Jean had seen the tragedy spelled out in newspapers before: first the dog, then the boy, then the parents, and everyone but the dog drowns. There was nobody to help. Marvin was back at the campsite, out of yelling range, and how could he help, anyway? The waves were huge and crashing against an outcropping of jagged rocks. She couldn't call anyone. The closest cell service was miles from there. She screamed at Maverick to stay out of the water and then held him helplessly as they watched their dog struggle, then relax, as she washed out to sea.

So, Jean was looking forward to once again

having an infant ticket to join the mommy groups dawdling along the path, safely above the beach, chatting and pausing to look out at the sea. That was, if she could make time.

"Hi!" Wynn said, getting in line behind them. Jean hugged her, leaning slightly to one side so they could get a hug in around Jean's belly.

"Hi Wynn! So glad you could make it! This is my friend Kimberly. Kimberly, Wynn," Jean introduced her new friend to her old one.

"Everyone calls me Kim," Kim reached her hand out to shake Wynn's but Wynn was already leaning in for a hug so Kim shifted gears and reciprocated the warmer welcome. Jean looked at her friends embracing. They couldn't be more opposite if you considered appearances alone. Where Kim looked sophisticated, Wynn looked homey. Today Kim was wearing black leather boots trimmed in some poor animal's fur, a tight black shirt that accented her baby bump, and yoga pants that made her appear even taller and more slender than she was, if that was possible. Wynn was thin, too (pregnancy aside, Jean was well aware that she was the fatty of this group by at least twenty pounds), but Wynn looked like the anything-comfortable stay-at-home mom she was: brown UGGs with a few years of wear on them, loose jeans, and a black Santa Cruz sweatshirt with the classic epithet of mothers: a smear of white baby goo on the shoulder.

"Isn't it cold outside? This is supposed to be June in sunny Santa Cruz, not San Francisco!" Wynn said.

It was cold out, but Santa Cruz was funny like that. It was often cold in the morning, then sunny and warm until evening appeared. "Dress in layers," locals advised houseguests. But the thick-as-pea-soup fog was a little unusual, probably due to an early summer heatwave farther inland in the Silicon Valley.

"Yeah! Someone needs to give that fog a map!" Jean agreed.

"Well, it's toasty in here... what are you having?" Kim asked, looking over the case of treats. Jean was staring at this perfect, petite chocolate cake for one, with a strawberry cut and spread into a fan across the top. Usually she stuck with something a little less decadent, like one of those itty bitty lemon meringue tarts, but nothing else looked chocolaty enough. She decided she would risk the heartburn and go for it.

"Yeah, forget chit chat about the weather, Kim, let's get to the point!" Wynn teased. Wynn had left baby Julien with his dad, but she was still bouncing a little. Jean remembered doing that. Once she was spacing out and bouncing in line at the bank, sans baby, when she suddenly noticed that a stranger had been staring at her for several minutes. She joked that she had to pee, and then quickly gave up her place in line to go hide in the bathroom. Looking at Wynn, Jean had no idea why she was so embarrassed. Wynn just looked like a beautiful woman who enjoyed the self-stimulation of a little bouncing.

"I'm having that pink macaroon sandwich thingie

with the cream and raspberries," Kim said.

"Didn't you get that last time?" Jean asked. She had.

"Don't be questioning a pregnant woman about what she wants to eat!" Wynn reprimanded, and they all giggled. "It's a non-fat vanilla steamer for me. Unlike you preggos, I am supposed to be lightening up on the scale."

"Whatever, Wynn. You fit into your pre-pregnancy jeans after, like what, four months?" Jean asked.

"Don't tell me you're one of those mystical women who survive without caffeine, Wynn." Kim interrupted. "When Dr. Phyllis said my daily cup of Christian crank wouldn't harm the baby I whooped with joy right there in her office."

"Well, I have a different definition of harm. Anyway, the last thing I need is to hype Julien up with caffeinated boob juice. After Oliver's colic, I recognize my great fortune to have a mellow baby and I'd like to keep him that way," Wynn defended. Julien did seem like a dream baby. Jean had hung out with Wynn about three times since they'd first met, and she had only heard Julien cry that first day at the playground.

They placed their orders and went to sit on the bench seats, placing their little silver posts with the numbers attached on the table where their treats would soon reside.

"So Paul asked me again if I was going to start thinking about going back to work now that our last baby is over six months old," Wynn started in, the tone of her voice indicating how ridiculous she thought her husband was being. Wynn hadn't worked since before she had Oliver, almost four years earlier. Her husband wanted her to start really thinking about it. Wynn had no idea what she wanted to do. Although she had a degree in political science, her pre-baby resume consisted of mostly waitressing and coordinating volunteer beach clean ups, both of which seemed a big step backwards from motherhood. She had already told Jean that she wanted to stay home at least until both children were in school.

"He doesn't understand why I don't just figure out what I want to do and start looking at job listings, as if I can just pick up where I left off before I had Oliver. I tried to explain that physically and psychologically, you have to give yourself up, actually allow yourself to be transformed into a different human in order to have the baby. There is no way around it and no going back." Wynn paused and then winced a little. "Except for adopting...sorry..." she said to Jean.

"Don't worry, you have to do plenty of transforming yourself during the adoption process. Anyway, I get your point about having to surrender to a new self. Look at me." Jean said, pointing to her swollen body. Her belly button was so erect it looked like one of those turkey timers that pop up. Jean was still two weeks from her due date, but her belly button definitely said "done."

"Thanks. Well, I was reminding him that when I was pregnant, I spent the majority of each day wishing I could either sleep or puke," she continued.

"Oh, I totally get that," Kim interrupted. "My first trimester I felt exhausted and nauseous as fuck most of the day, but I couldn't sleep through the night and I never puked. Except for one time when I forced myself, but it didn't help. Oh, I'm sorry, was that TMI?" she asked.

"Honey, we're all moms here, nothing is TMI anymore," Wynn reassured her. "Anyway, I felt stripped of so many important aspects of myself. I had been sexy, beautiful, smart, fun....and then none of those adjectives applied. They'd been replace with my new, all-consuming adjective: pregnant. Then—"

"You're still fun." Jean interrupted, then regretted interrupting. Wynn was trying to get a point across and she didn't want Wynn to think she was missing it.

Wynn smiled, "Thanks, Jean. But I mean the 'going out to a concert' kind of fun, not the 'I can still laugh at myself' kind of fun."

"I know," Kim said. "We just don't want you to come down on yourself too hard. But, I feel exactly the same way. It's like we contort ourselves to go through our own birth canal, and when we come out on the other side we are different. This is my first baby, but I can already feel the changes in me. Not just my body, but my psyche. I used to love to go to concerts, too. Ron and I went all the time, and I thought I was just that type of person. But now, I haven't been out past nine in six months, and I haven't missed it one bit! I can't even imagine wanting to go."

It was the truth, too. Back when Kim and Jean worked at the firm together, Kim was the most happening woman Jean knew. She and Ron were always going to some art gallery opening or funk concert up in San Francisco. Jean used to feel a little jealous of Kim on Mondays because she'd tell her about some fabulous new sushi place she'd discovered over the weekend, and Jean would have nothing but the fact that you can get sugar crystals to form on string, which was her favorite one of Maverick's science projects until the ants discovered it.

"What comes out on the other side *is* a new person. Her name is Mommy," Jean offered, but she felt a little hollow saying it. Looking at Kim and Wynn, she wondered if she could relate to these women. Neither of them had their first baby until their 30s. Jean was a mother before she was an adult, and although it was a major change from being a sort of wild girl in high school to being a mother and wife, that identity crisis was so long ago it was hard to remember. Kim and Wynn had so many years to build up a whole childless identity. Jean could hardly imagine what it would be like to be an adult that didn't have anyone to care for but themselves. They must have so much time.

"That is what I'm saying! After the baby is out you have to reinvent yourself all over again while you settle into all of your new routines as 'Mommy'. It takes a while to map out who this new person is, what she likes, what she wants...and the whole process so rattles and shakes you, and you work so hard at just submitting to it all, that it isn't easy to figure yourself out once there is an opening to be something more than 'Mommy'," Wynn finished and looked at them, hoping for validation. Jean gave her what she hoped was an understanding nod, but inside she was still struggling to relate. Jean had been a mom for twenty years, but didn't have much experience at being "just" a mom.

Jean looked over at Kim, as pregnant as she was she wasn't a mother yet. And, Jean guessed, Kim was probably even less likely to relate to the issues of a stay-at-home mom. Kim's plan, Jean knew, was to take the twelve weeks California graciously offers new mothers, and then head straight back to the firm. She didn't seem to be having any of the existential angst that Jean was suffering. While Jean felt almost catatonic at the at the looming decision she had to make between getting childcare or giving away clients, Kim had already lined up some high-priced Montessori daycare where they spoke Spanish half the day and listened to classical music. She was smiling and nodding Wynn on though, Kim was cool like that.

Wynn was so wrapped up in her crisis that she didn't notice that the other women were not on the same page. "It's like I run this marathon called motherhood, where my only focus is on the baby and the house. And I love it, but it's so consuming. It takes all my effort just to keep up, so there is no way I can just instantly jump back into being my pre-mother self. That person, I think, went through a painful molting during my first pregnancy and those early months of mothering. Whoever I was is no longer and who I will be outside of the mother box is someone I have to form, brick by brick, out of mud and hay in the wilderness." Wynn looked a little distraught. Luckily, their treats arrived, delivered by a young woman sporting that punk rockabilly look with the dyed black hair, thick bangs, and a tattoo of two red cherries on the underside of her wrist (which must have really stung). All three women happily dug in, and the sweet sugar melting in their mouths also melted the tension.

"Well, Paul is just going to have to deal with the fact that this process isn't going to happen overnight. You are a busy mother of two boys and it is going to take you a while to even recognize moments you can take for yourself. Then, once you see them, you'll learn to grab them and use them to figure out who you are apart from your babies," Kim said, showing more understanding than Jean had given her credit for. And, suddenly, Jean also remembered the exact feeling Wynn was describing. For Jean it wasn't so much about needing the time to find herself in a career, but about doing all the other things she should do to take care of herself. When was the last time she "had time" to go to the gym that automatically deducted $50.00 from her checking account every month like a penance?

"Yes, Wynn, Kim is right. When you have a little one to take care of it is so hard to see the windows of opportunity to take care of yourself, because those windows are not determined by your own sensibilities. You go to the bathroom when you have a spare moment to go, not any old time your body wants to," she said and they all laughed, even Kim, who had a demanding child called a law career for years before she got pregnant with a human one.

"I guess this is the process of weaning," Wynn sighed. "First you release them from your womb, then later their desire for food slowly releases them from your breast. And as they release from you, you are left there alone, looking around for something useful to do."

"Until one day they fly out of the nest and go to college!" Jean snorted, thinking of Maverick, who was only a couple hours away at the University of San Francisco, but light-years away from her breast. And yet, she still had a visceral memory of how badly he wanted her milk. He used to attack her like a little tiger, his latch so forceful that her foot would inadvertently kick out, slamming anything in its path. Her parents and Marvin would laugh— "Now there is a little fellow who knows what he wants!"

"It's work to find yourself again, Wynn, but it's good work," Kim said. "Think of the women who aren't able to formulate a happy individual self again. My mother wasn't able to pull it off and you should see her; her children weaned, moved away, and there she stayed, floating around her empty nest with nothing to do but find creative ways to be grumpy with my dad, and cajoling us kids to visit more often." Jean had never heard Kim talk about her mom before, and now her compassion for Wynn and obvious determination not to be a homemaker made sense. It was funny how simple people really were, Jean thought. Shrinks must just laugh.

"Hey! Don't trash moms who want their children home!" Jean said in mock protest. "Maverick hasn't visited in a month, and if he doesn't show up soon, I'm going to cancel this whole college/growing up thing and just lock him in his room."

"You should count your blessings, Jean. So many boys in Santa Cruz grow up to be surfers living in their parents' backyard. Maverick is living up to his name by doing something different." Wynn laughed her easy laugh, the stress of her life buoyed in the traditional way: by the friendship of women. "Well, the weaning has begun for me, and the windows of opportunity to take another look at myself *are* slowly appearing. I mean, look, here I am, hanging out with you without any baby. This would have seemed impossible only a month ago. But Julien has started on solids and, I guess, he doesn't need me constantly."

"Maybe Paul offered to take him as a way to convince you that you do have a little time," Jean suggested. "Today Julien can live without you for an hour. In a bit it will be four hours, then a whole day. In a year, or whenever you wean, he'll be able to survive the night without you."

"I think Paul just wanted to score some points so he could get laid." Wynn rolled her eyes.

"Hey, I have a question, girls. Do you have sex in the last trimester?" Kim looked around conspiratorially, "and, if you don't, do you give blow jobs? Ron has suggested that this might be a great alternative."

"Alternative to what? Fucking a wife as big as a horse?'" Jean laughed, hoping that Kim was not offended because, really, Jean was so much bigger than Kim. "Not that Marvin has a choice in the matter. When I am pregnant, I am so horny I actually orgasm in my sleep!"

"I think he was saying as an alternative to driving over to San Jose and ordering out for skinny sex," Kim replied. "I think he's starting to panic. I totally missed the horny boat with this pregnancy. I feel nauseous any time I'm not eating, and I seriously think the rocking motion of sex would make me puke."

"Eww! Well, I guess you have your solution then!" Wynn offered, "Sounds like your choice is between skanky hooker, vomit in bed, or a tablespoon of nutritious bit-o-man honey—which might have the added benefit of keeping nausea at bay because, after all, it is something to eat..."

Kim laughed so hard the bite of meringue cookie she had just put into her mouth came flying out.

"And so convenient, too!" Jean joked, "You don't even have to get up and search through the fridge—

it's right there next to you in bed."

"Okay! Okay! Change the subject," Kim insisted, then cleared her throat loudly with an: "Ah-hem!" and looked pointedly at Jean. "Jean, how are you doing? Have you heard anything more from Maya? Is she still coming?"

Just the name sent a cold chill down Jean's spine. "She hasn't called for a week, but the last time I spoke to her she said she was still coming," Jean groaned.

"What does she want?" Kim asked, ever the lawyer. She had more than once over the past couple weeks reminded Jean that she had nothing to fear. All the adoption papers were in order. It was just a visit, nothing more. Nothing more *and nothing less*, Jean kept thinking.

"I don't know. I hope to God that she isn't planning on moving here. I'm already so freaked out about how this new baby will come between Sienna and me. The last thing I need is for her to feel like I'm not her real mom, or that this new baby is my real baby. I knew Maya would show up someday, but why now, Lord?" Jean looked up at the ceiling and pleaded her last sentence to the sky, just in case anyone up there was listening.

"You know, this could be a blessing in disguise," Wynn said.

"What? No, this is a curse. I wouldn't give up Sienna for the world, so I'm happy that Maya exists, but her showing up now, right as I'm about to have another baby? This is definitely Satan's little fickle finger poking into my life to remind me that if I wasn't so easy as a teen I'd have been a better example for my son and would have a normal family."

"Well, I've heard you say 'normal family' more than once, but what is that, anyway? There is so much pain in this world, and you have a house full of love. You and Marvin are straight out of some Norman Rockwell painting you're so cute with each other, and Sienna is a doll who I'm sure will continue to feel very, very loved," Kim said.

Jean remembered her voice from just last week when Jean was obsessing about the same thing. "You know, you're always so hard on yourself. Yes, you had Maverick when you were a teen and yes, Maverick followed suit and had Sienna. But look what you got out of it! You are young enough to not only enjoy, but also raise your granddaughter. Look at me; I'm thirty-five, and if this baby follows the pattern I'm setting I'll be *seventy* when my first grandchild is born. My father died when he was sixty-nine, so I might not even live to see a grandchild! Your family's timing is a little weird in our culture, but it's not so unusual around the world or throughout human history. And maybe it's the better way."

"But, you got to have a whole life before babies; you traveled, you had a career..." Jean had protested.

"You have a great career, working your own schedule by yourself, and I bet that you were way more focused going to law school at 28 than I was at

22. Now I'm at a firm, and sure I make money, but I have crazy billable hours and only two months' maternity leave because I couldn't imagine going out on my own like you have." Jean had to agree. She did have it good. But that was last week. Jean needed cheering up again.

"But, Kim, I remember what it's like to have a baby. I'm going to be exhausted. Sienna is a doll, but she is a doll that needs a ton of attention. I'm not sure how it's going to work," Jean responded.

"Yeah, Jean, really, listen to us," Wynn interjected. "Oliver wasn't adopted, but I am going through the same thing you are. All mothers feel on some level like they are abandoning their older child when they have another—*that* is normal. You just probably didn't go through it when you adopted Sienna because you were helping Maverick out and, anyway, he was so much older. We do have to divide our attentions when we have another child and, yes, they might lose a smidgen of mother's love, but they benefit, too. They get to have a sibling and that is a gift that they'll have their whole life—even after you are dead and gone."

Wynn stood up and gathered her things to go, her big hour off almost up. Jean had to get going too. It was almost ten thirty, and she had to finish drafting Ms. Pointier's estate documents before she came in at two. The woman had been married three times and had a whole menagerie of children, stepchildren, grandchildren and step-grandchildren that had earned varying degrees of her affection.

Jean guessed Kim was right, that there was no real normal anymore. Maybe Wynn was right too, she thought. She actually was a little surprised to learn that Wynn felt like she was abandoning Oliver. The woman had dedicated her whole life to her children. Oliver was three, and Jean was not sure he even knew the word "babysitter." Feeling inadequate was just part of the mother job description.

"Okay, I hear both of you. I guess I need to find the silver lining in all of this." Jean stacked up their empty plates to put in the bin near the door.

"Yeah, maybe she'll show up and be your nanny!" Kim said, and then reached back to pull her long blond hair out of the maternity-style black wool pea coat she'd just put on.

"Hah!" Jean laughed.

CHAPTER TEN

WHEN PEOPLE HAD described their cross-country road trips to Jesse the amount of time spent talking about Nebraska had little relation to how much time one actually must spend crossing the state, end to end. Jack Kerouac, in particular, had not properly prepared Jesse for the mix of stunning beauty and utter banality that comes with mile after mile, hour after hour, of flat.

Looking over the endless plains, Jesse couldn't help imagine proud Indians, with full feather headdresses and red paint highlighting lean, muscular builds, riding at full gallop to herd buffalo or trample half-starved explorers.

He thought of the settlers traveling slowly along rutted paths in a long line of covered wagons, doing just as he was doing now: roaming through other people's land with a half baked plan to trade everything they knew in exchange for the hope of a golden future. Go West! Jesse could hear the beating of their hearts. Looking out his window he knew something they'd forgotten to mention in his fourth grade history books. Crossing the Great Plains may have been long, and hot, and difficult, but it offered something for the traveler that guaranteed enough hope to persevere: a sky so grand even the biggest dream had ample room to soar. This wasn't just the Great Plains, this was the Endless Skyway.

The tremendous mountains and valleys of Nebraska float in the air. From his seat whizzing down the highway, Jesse could see cumulous clouds stacked as tall as New York skyscrapers and a soft fuzz of stratus clouds that seemed to shade hundreds of miles before seeping off to where the blue sky kissed the green fields on the horizon.

In Nebraska, the vast holds the monotonous and the monotonous affords the vast. This was the promise and delivery of any monogamous relationship, thought Jesse. You agree to have the same, over and over and over again, but the stability below allows for great amounts of room in the heavens above. With your basic primal needs met or eased through the sharing of resources and bodies, perhaps there would be more time to explore the spiritual experience.

Jesse turned to look at Maya, who was so absorbed in some politician's memoirs that she was missing everything. Would they have a serious, monogamous relationship? Could he enjoy the long, straight road, with its promise of rising above carnal need to the heavens beyond? He imagined them together, a marital seal supporting their earthly selves while they endeavored to reach nirvana at some ashram in India. But, his mind kept drifting back to the image of half-naked Native Americans, their sweat glistening under the exposed Nebraska sky, their bodies quivering with each pound of those mighty hoses' hoofs.

"Well, this is where I get off," announced the middle aged office worker named John that had picked them up from an on ramp near Jada's house. He pulled his old model Corolla off the highway and pointed to a Safeway sign. "Do you want to go there?"

"That's perfect. Thanks so much. We really appreciate the ride," Jesse said. He had hoped to get a little farther, but you take what you can get when you're hitchhiking—and you remember to be thankful. A short ride is an opportunity to practice gratitude.

"You know, since you're heading west you kids should check out my buddy Hawk's place near Moab, Utah. He runs an Echinacea farm down there and always needs extra hands. Usually has a group of kids like you hanging around."

"Wow. Thanks John. We were looking for something like this." Jesse took Hawk's telephone number. Being polite pays off!

The automatic doors of the grocery store swished open to invite them to trade the fragrant air of the open plains for the pungent mix of Clorox and Freon coolant. They hadn't eaten since breakfast at Jada's so they made a beeline for the pre-cooked meal section. Maya slowly picked over the salad bar, complaining about the lettuce. "How many gallons of petroleum did it take to truck this stuff from California?" The question was obviously rhetorical, so Jesse just continued scooping barbecue pork from the hot bar, his spoon cracking through the fatty film that had congealed on the surface of the serving bucket. It had been six hours since breakfast and he was starving. Jesse intended to fully enjoy his time at the Safeway in Grand Island, Nebraska.

"Americans think that they have a God-given right to spinach no matter where they choose to live. Climate be dammed. It totally reminds me of when we lived in Kauai, and the hipsters would walk around guzzling coconut water out of a plastic bottle. They'd act like they just discovered this amazing drink and start raving to you 'it's, like, totally full of potassium,' completely ignoring that they were putting their own health before the environment!"

Maya's impressions of stoned neo-hippies was dead-on and usually made Jesse laugh, but his friends and he had really been into coconut water lately. Her mocking was starting to seem like a superiority trip. He focused on the savory collection he was amassing on his plate, piling fried rice on top of the pork. "It was so ridiculous, Jesse, I'm telling you. These people, who would rather cut off their right arm than be seen drinking a Coke, were going through several coconut waters a day—and nobody there really believes they recycle on that island. And the whole time there were trees bulging with coconuts, just swaying in the wind!" Maya finished with an exasperated huff, and then sprinkled a scoop full of chopped nuts on top of the offending spinach.

"That is why I stick with good ol' Adam's Ale from my trusty Nalgene," Jesse said, leaning sideways slightly to expose the scratched-up old bottle stuck in the side pocket of his backpack. He didn't feel like arguing. He was tired. The fold-out couch at Jada's was totally uncomfortable, and his back hurt. It was only two in the afternoon, but he was already debating whether they should get a motel room or try to make it closer to Denver tonight. I should call my uncle, Jesse thought, and let him know either way. The best thing about hitchhiking was that you never know what will happen, but it was also the worst thing about it. Jesse looked over at Maya. It was the same with people. Their best traits were also their worst. Maya was whip-smart, with a super strong personality—that was sexy. But, he was realizing, it can also be tiring. Like today. They weren't around Jada and her baby issues anymore. Couldn't they just eat without the political commentary?

"You know those old Nalgene bottles are toxic, don't you? They haven't sold that kind in years," Maya noted.

"Makes me strong!" Jesse joked, and set down his plate to beat his chest like a gorilla. Maya laughed, but Jesse could tell that she was in a bad mood. What was she going to complain about next?

After Maya finally assembled her salad (guilt, dressing and all) and Jesse had a Styrofoam plate full of steaming animal goodness (that had surely suffered a miserable life before being doused in tangy finger-sucking sauce), they went to the counter so Jesse could pay. At first Jesse had really liked how Maya was so easygoing about letting him pay for everything. So many women insist on paying for themselves.

Of course, Jesse knew that women were fully capable beings that can take care of themselves just as well or better than a man, his mom was proof of that. But it just felt right to Jesse to take care of a woman and the feeling stuck, in spite of the logic. One time while arguing over the bill with a female friend of his he pointed out that if women were really only earning $0.70 to a man's dollar then men should be obligated to make up for this by paying for dinner. He got laid that night, and rightfully so.

Maya wasn't so concerned. As they sat down, Jesse thought he should lighten their mood with a little teasing. Or maybe he just thought poking at her would lighten his. "So, if you're so righteous, how is it that you don't have any problem with letting me pay for everything?" Jesse said in what he hoped was a jokey, lighthearted tone. He didn't really want her to feel uncomfortable. He did offer to pay for the trip, but maybe he did want her to realize that she wasn't so perfect. "Usually women get so pissy about their self-dignity if I try to pay for them on dinner dates."

"Maybe if our society wasn't so stuck on the idea that money equals self-worth there wouldn't be so many silly arguments over the little black folder delivered with the 'take your time' lie," she responded, sneering a little as she repeated the line she knew Jesse had said to so many people at his job. Was she making fun of him? "Think about it; major societal problems result from the dignity equals money bullshit. Even if they inherited it all, the wealthy think that the simple fact that they have riches proves that they are more worthy than poor people to have them. Did you know that early Americans thought that you could identify the people favored by God by how much wealth they have? Henry Ford actually bragged that he was doing his part to prove to the world that God loves Americans best by making Fords affordable." Jesse sat back. What had he gotten himself into? Now they were going to have to discuss the class divide throughout lunch? He looked around, but this time Maya seemed to be tensing up without any baby in sight.

"There's a basic rule of economics," Maya went

on, "one person can only create so much wealth. The biggest struggle in any society is between the people who desire more wealth than they can themselves create, and the laborers who aren't so excited to hand it over. So it's stolen from them, on the front end through low wages, or on the back end through taxes or junk goods. And after it has consolidated in the hands of the rich and been passed down a few generations, they just assume that it is their divine right to have it, and don't question who really earned it."

Now Jesse was annoyed. He may not be as conservative as his mom, but he was starting to realize what mom meant when she said that college liberals go way too far with this socialist bullshit. Not that he could define "socialist" other than that it was someone who hates rich people, but he did have a strong desire to put Maya in her place. "Don't you think you're going a little too far? Getting rich is the American dream. I'm definitely not on the path to become a CEO or anything, but I'm not going to judge someone who has worked for it and leaves an inheritance for his children."

"The myth that CEOs have worked hard enough to earn all that money is part of the problem, Jesse. The reason why our economy is so fucked right now is because the big banks argued that they have to pay the mucky-mucks millions every year; that those jerks are worth the money. This entitlement belief completely disregards the fact that bank money is generated by millions of hard workers, who also deserve to benefit from the fruits of their labor," Maya lectured. This was totally ridiculous, Jesse thought. She was actually going to ruin lunch with this.

Jesse started to dig in to his steaming plate of BBQ meets Chinese delight and, after the first bites; he decided to throw an olive branch. "Maya, you don't have to get all worked up. I'm totally fine paying for lunch and whatever. I invited you on this trip. Let's just eat. Okay?"

"Jesse, that apathy is exactly what allows them to do what they do! The poor and middle class just sit around eating fatty takeout food or imported spinach salads while the wealthy fleece them. The other day I went to a lecture in Georgetown about how these private companies are paid millions of dollars to do things that supposedly support our troops in foreign wars. Things like running cafeterias. They charge way more than our government would spend if it did the jobs itself, but who pays for it? We do! It's a total scam on the government, but it is even more a scam on the middle class, because the middle class pays more on taxes than the rich do."

Jesse seriously doubted that Maya had ever paid taxes. He tried again. "Maya, I'm not apathetic. I'm just trying to eat my lunch. I know all about how much taxes suck. My mom bitches about taxes and the government all the time. But I'm sure you're wrong about the middle class paying more than rich people. Taxes are based on how much income you earn and anyway, I really don't feel like arguing. Just drop it, okay?"

"But, Jesse, you're wrong about taxes. The IRS taxes people on their income at a high rate. And yes, the rate increases depending on your income; but the wealthy have huge loopholes that exempt most of their earnings from those rates. And big corporations are even worse. After they take advantage of all of the tax deductions and loopholes, if they still owe the IRS, they are allowed to just give Uncle Sam an IOU and then deduct it later when their earnings aren't so high. Imagine if your mom were allowed to just tell the IRS, 'I owe you five grand this year but I won't pay you because I think next year or the year after that might be a hard year for me.' You know our government considers corporations people? So much for equality. Clearly some 'people' are treated better than others." Maya looked at Jesse defiantly, as if she actually expected him to bend down and thank her for her great pearls of wisdom. Oh heavenly Maya, you are so wise and I'm just some dumb asshole. Thank you, thank you for explaining the ways of the world.

Jesse had enough. He stood up, put his backpack on, and took his half-eaten plate of food. "You know, Maya, I don't really give a shit about taxes right now. I told you to drop it, but it's like you're obsessed with showing how righteous you are and there is no point. Why don't you find someone else to squash? I'm going outside." The Safeway had a few tables outside, sectioned off from the sidewalk with low cement walls, but it was cold and empty except for a black Labrador tied to a chair. That was fine; Jesse wanted to be alone anyway. He petted the Lab and sat down at the next table. He ate a couple more bites of his food, but it wasn't hot anymore so he threw the rest away. There was nothing more disgusting than cold hot bar food. Now he was hungry and fuming. What had gotten into Maya? She was so sweet, but it was like that time with Jada unleashed some crazy femi-nazi and now she was on a tirade. Honestly, he saw signs of her being political before, but it seemed cute, not all bitchy.

Maybe she had PMS. Growing up as the only male in the house, Jesse knew about periods. His mom would get on a huge tirade about some mess he'd made or some chore he hadn't done. Trish would start sobbing about a guy and then get furious with Jesse for not "getting it." It was like clockwork every month, but they always acted surprised. They would actually laugh about the whole thing afterward when their period would show up. Like "Oh, oops I'm sorry I freaked out all last night, I guess it was just PMS, ha ha." But God save him if he ever suggested they were picking on him because of hormones.

Being the youngest person and the only male in the household, Jesse learned at an early age not to argue with women. Or anyone hell-bent on being right. If his sister or his mom started in on him he would go hide in his room. If he wasn't out partying with his best buddy, Slaven, on the weekend, he was usually hiding in his room anyway, playing music and video games on the Internet. Maya had seemed to be the polar opposite of his mother and Trish when they'd met. Different politics, same fucking hormones, Jesse thought now. How do men ever find one that they actually want to marry? Jesse, really, couldn't imagine even wanting one as a roommate.

He needed to call his uncle to let him know that they would be there soon, maybe even tomorrow, if the hitchhiking gods agreed. But he didn't have a phone, and he didn't want to go back in to use Maya's. He had been so excited to throw himself completely into this adventure; he'd even given up his cell phone. These days people travel all over the world with their cell phones, but he didn't want the ties and distained the modernity of it.

Jesse had gotten into the unusual habit of writing pen and paper letters the year before when Slaven spent the summer in upstate New York to be part of some art collective a girl had invited him to join. They had decided to subvert of the dominant paradigm by exchanging actual paper and pen letters rather than e-mails while he was gone, and they'd continued even after he returned. Since they were both angling to be famous writers, they reasoned that it was good practice. Maybe it was, but it was also easier to discuss real, deep feelings on paper... so much so that it wasn't uncommon for them to have a whole letter exchange about how broken up one of them was over some girl, but never talk about it in person, even though they saw each other almost every day.

He didn't want to bring a phone because he didn't want the distraction, he had written to Slaven before he left DC. "It sounds cheesy to explain," he'd admitted, "but I want to use this road trip to enter into a world where I don't have to self-monitor how cheesy I sound. People in other places, talking about other lives, will distract me from the Now that I am seeking. I know if I keep up with the happenings in Adam's Morgan I will return sooner than I want. I will be roped back in, the phone acting as a tether, tugging me softly and constantly with a whisper about the fun I am missing back home. But if I stay in the moment: meet people, see places, love them, and then say good-bye, I can really settle into myself and the world I inhabit at the moment, in the moment. The world I choose to create with the myriad of decisions I will make along the way, both minuscule and grand. Rather than greener grass down the road, I will seek only the beacon of light shining out from the depths of my own soul. And to do this, I must loosen myself from the self-cannibalism that comes with the constant narration of my own life online, and even talking to friends."

Jesse was proud of how Beat-like he'd sounded in his letter, which was the point of the road trip and the letter. Mostly, it was working. Already, Jesse noticed that the people who had been so important to him in DC were fading from his daily thoughts. Except that he would way rather have Slaven on this road trip than Maya right now. Jesse considered getting out his notebook and writing Slaven something nuanced and insightful on how much women suck, but then he had a revelation.

Okay, maybe not a revelation in the sense of huge and life-changing, but it did occur to him that sitting miserably outside of some nondescript grocery store deep in the Midwest was exactly the sort of misadventure one needed to get depressed. And no one could ever hope to be great without some depression and misery in their past, right? Bad moments were a necessary part of the experience. This moment, Jesse decided, was just a bad moment. And as far as bad goes, especially compared with forced labor camps and other horrors that exist outside of Jesse's middle-class, American life, this wasn't really even that bad; just annoying, really. He went on this road trip to experience life, the whole spectrum, Jesse reminded himself. Road trips were supposed to have uncomfortable, annoying moments. Wasn't that part of the package? Well, here it was. This thought cheered Jesse up tremendously. Or at least enough to go back inside and borrow Maya's phone.

CHAPTER ELEVEN

THEY MADE IT from Jada's house to Jesse's uncle's in less than 30 hours, but it took six rides to get there. Uncle Jim seemed pissed when they showed up after midnight. He answered the door in old striped pajama bottoms and complained that only criminals were up at that hour. Jesse knew that he should have booked them into a hotel, but he was feeling cheap. That Safeway argument had put him in the mood to save his money for a girl he liked better.

Uncle Jim wasn't into the idea of Jesse taking the car on a road trip. He kept saying he thought Jesse's mom expected him to drive the car straight back. He had probably imagined his kid sister's son was some normal-looking kid from the 'burbs that would keep the old Honda nicely polished for a daily commute to work. Instead, Jesse showed up in grungy clothes, a big gold hoop through his nostrils, traveling with a woman who wore black nail polish, and a plan to use the car for a wild spree to California.

Maya didn't help, either. She noticed photographs on the wall of Jim with dead mountain lions and immediately launched into a discussion about hunting for meat vs. play. She wasn't rude or anything, but you could actually see the good intentions Jim had about giving Jesse the car draining out of him.

It was so awkward that they left before breakfast and headed west into the mountains on I70. Jesse had planned on pulling over and having celebratory sex with Maya as soon as they had their own car, but he was in such a sour mood that he just turned on the radio and drove.

There was an early morning fog in the foothills, like the kind you drink coffee in the morning to dispel from your brain, but as they climbed up the steep Rocky Mountains the air grew cold and clear. The cold in the air reflected the cold in the car. They had barely said a word to each other since they left Jesse's uncle's. The world of trees was soon far below and they were traveling now, exposed, with only hard ice and rock for company. The unsympathetic blue of the sky, the sun glaring at them through thin air—nothing felt protected, nothing felt warm. Jesse had the distinct feeling that he wasn't supposed to be there. Humans, with their soft naked flesh and delicate skeletons, are not supposed to be on rugged mountaintops. Jesse had the strong sensation of wanting to be somewhere else.

The interstate wound its way, sometimes turning sharply to move with the landscape and other times brutally forcing its way through with tunnels and slices. The entire pass was a tribute to the power of dynamite and man's insistence on ramming himself into nature's glory. Jesse started wondering if he'd been forcing a path with Maya. Was there anything natural and real between them or was their relationship just some emptiness that he'd dynamited into existence because he needed a path through his own fear to travel alone? They rounded a curve and Jesse had to swerve a little to avoid a small pile of dirty snow that had tumbled off the cliffs above. A cold, dirty mess that needed to be removed.

He really didn't want to get into another fight, but it was starting to feel like Maya wasn't the person he had thought she was and he felt a sudden urge to figure out just who, exactly, was in the car with him. "You know, Maya, I've never met anyone like you. And I know you're super unique, but sometimes you sound, and I really don't want you to take this the wrong way, but, I don't know, just like every other angry college liberal in DC," Jesse said.

"The problem here isn't my politics, Jesse," Maya

said leisurely, without turning her head from the view of the green valley far below, which was still slightly obscured by a soft haze. "You're upset because the first few days we spent together we basically had sex constantly, and now it's been two days and you're irritable." She wasn't wrong. Jesse's penis swelled a little at her bluntness.

"No, really, I'm just trying to get to know you. I mean, here we are, more than halfway across the country, climbing a mountain together, and we still don't know each other all that well."

"Well, I don't know if I can help you there. I've been feeling pretty confused the last few days. I think I'm angry, but I'm not sure who I'm angry at. I don't know. I think I was rude to Jada, which sucks. I'm sorry about lecturing you at Safeway too. I'm not sure what is going on with me. I feel pissed-off for no reason. I'm starting to wonder if I should even be on this trip. Maybe I should have kept that internship. I spend so much time wanting to live a normal life, but, I guess, I can't sustain it. It's too boring for me. I just gravitate elsewhere. I mean, look at me. I was offered a prestigious internship, but what did I do? Go on a cross-country road trip with some guy I met in a club. It's like a self-sabotage, except I don't know if what I'm sabotaging is really the self I want anyway."

A tumble of small rocks fell onto the highway in front of them and Jesse looked up in time to see a mountain goat, its horns curled into a mighty crown, jump nimbly from a jagged outcropping to the relative safety of a large boulder. Maya turned to look at Jesse, her eyes wanting to confirm that he'd heard her, that he *saw* her.

"Maybe it's your true nature crying out. I would die of boredom if I had to go to college and hang out with all of those upwardly mobiles," Jesse offered.

"But I didn't think I would feel like that. I was so excited about going to college. I thought I would finally find my people in DC. I had this image of people standing around Greek pillars, debating big ideas. Studying history, philosophy, economics in the universities and then jumping in with the government or a non-profit to roll up their sleeves and really change things. Instead, it mostly feels like I'm hanging out with party-hungry, sex-starved babies. And the whole DC job process is greased by 'who-you-know,' but it's hard to 'know' anyone if you can't stand hanging out with them at the frat parties." Jesse wanted to be supportive, but he wasn't sure what Maya was thinking. Maybe he was jaded because he grew up near DC, but you have to be pretty naive to think that this country is run by a bunch of Roman philosophers trying to save the world.

"I think if you start down a road pretending to be someone that you aren't, you won't like where you end up. I know this guy, he runs an art gallery near Adam's Morgan. He used to be a partner at one of the huge law firms downtown. He's gay, but he told me once that he pretended to be straight to get in with the right crowds in college, law school, and his first few years at the firm, thinking that once he 'made it' as a partner he would finally get to be himself. Well, it turned out that once he was a partner, he was expected to be a rainmaker, and that required certain country club memberships and golfing, and even more schmoozing with the people that he never wanted to spend time with in the first place," Jesse said.

Jesse had issues, but not being himself wasn't one of them. He was always pretty much Jesse. He had assumed that Maya was the same. She certainly didn't look like someone who was trying to fit in with "normal" society. He didn't want to break it to her, but with her long, loose hair, black nails, and clothes dominated by leather and lace, she looked a little more like a wannabe '80s punk rocker than a wannabe normal. It was funny how a person's self-perception can be so different from how others see them, and how so little of either have any basis in the reality of who that person really is.

"Yeah, I get why it's called a rat race," Maya said sadly. "Even if there is a little cheese here and there, there is always more race. I hate to admit it, but my parents warned me about it. Everyone I grew up with did. 'You'll never take down the master's house with the master's tools,' they said. But I thought it would be different for me. I know I don't belong with the society dropouts. I'm not interested in being alternative just to be alternative. But I'm obviously not going to be a lobbyist on K Street, either. I'm starting to think I don't fit in anywhere."

Jesse looked over at Maya, but he had a sinking feeling and didn't know what to say. If she had no idea who she was, he was even more confused. It was almost a little crazy the way women change so quickly, he thought. At first he was attracted to how self-confident she was, then at times she seemed a little too confident. Now she was just as insecure and uncertain about her future as he was. He was not sure what to make of her or how to help, or even if he wanted to help.

Instead of saying anything he might regret, he decided to let the view stand in for conversation. He pulled off the main highway to take the scenic route over Loveland Pass. They were so high up in the mountains now that the fields alongside the road still gripped large chunks of winter snow, holding their claim to an endless winter, facing off against small purple and yellow wildflowers fighting their way through. He stopped at a lookout with a large brown sign advertising the Continental Divide. Leaving Maya in the car, he climbed up on a short rock wall to take in the view. The air was so thin and crisp it couldn't hold the haze that had obscured the valley below. Everything was stark, unprotected. There were mountaintops jockeying for position as far as the eye could see and yet the entire effect was a stasis so profound that Jesse could feel the weight of an entire mountain under him. The wind whipping through Jesse's thin sweatshirt had passed through craggy cliffs, over miles of empty space without a drop of moisture or a single tree limb to soften its path. It smacked Jesse's cheeks with the cold, hard hand of someone who wanted him to suffer as it had.

Jesse could see his situation clearly. The silence between him and Maya was the sound of the empty pedestal. Maya, like so many women before her, had fallen off (gotten off?) the pedestal he had placed her on and now here they are at the Continental Divide, a place where two drops of water that fall as close to each other as he and Maya were siting might have destines that are oceans apart.

He glanced at Maya, who had followed him out of the car and onto the wall, but seated herself a few feet away. Her head was turned toward the view and she didn't look back. Maybe she was thinking the same thing. Maybe if he said it out loud she would be grateful, admit that she was not feeling it either, and they could figure out the logistics of getting out of this mess. Maybe she had a cousin in Reno or someplace and he could just drop her off, he thought hopefully. Yeah, right. If he said anything she would be upset, whether she was into him or not. She wouldn't have anywhere to go. She didn't have any money, her ego would be hurt, and he would have to drive a pissed-off woman to California and probably all the way back to DC, too. No, it was better to keep quiet. That way he could make the best of this situation and maybe get laid a few more times while he was figuring out how to get her out of his car.

Perhaps all this arguing and the lack of sex was a

blessing in disguise, Jesse decided. It was compelling him to look beyond his illusions and focus on his own life. He calculated that he was stuck with her for a couple more days at minimum till they got to California. After that, who knew? They'd talked about traveling around a bit—maybe even taking the southern route back East. But if things kept going in this direction, Jesse might put her on an airplane and drive home by himself. Or just stay in California. A jolt of fear passed through Jesse's body. Could he brave San Francisco alone?

CHAPTER TWELVE

AT JESSE'S REQUEST Maya called the guy in Utah with the Echinacea farm. Perhaps she sensed that she was on thin ice with Jesse because she didn't make anymore snarky remarks about suburban white boys reading Steinbeck. The guy's name was Hawk and he sounded as if he were expecting them.

"Oh yeah! Come on down, we're just outside of Moab, Utah. Plenty of room, just pitch your tent wherever. If all the lights are off when you get in, check the hot tub in the back. We're usually out there half the night. Just follow the music, man. Hey, did you buy any good weed in Colorado? I don't like that candy shit."

Traveling from the top of the Rocky Mountains to the desert plains of Utah trades dark, stark and hard for round, soft and rosy. Instead of chipping off in sharp edges, the rocks of Utah wear away tenderly, leaving pink sand and tall rounded pillars that spire upward like large penises stretched to meet lovers in the sky, tumbleweeds softly curled at their bases like fuzzy pubic hair. You can see the layers of millenniums past in their colorful ridges, where the wind releases dinosaur dust to tickle your nostrils.

Hawk's place was just south of Moab, a mountain biking town known for great swaths of grippy sandstone. By the time they arrived in Moab, Jesse was hungry and he needed gas so they decided to check out the town first. They found a little café with outdoor seating where they ordered bison meat hamburgers and watched young athlete-types and older hippies walk by, both dusted with the ubiquitous rainbow colored dirt. After dinner, they wondered around a bit to stretch their legs, stopping to admire the older western-style buildings and the tourist traps selling earth stained t-shirts, and then folded themselves back into the car to head over to Hawk's.

Hawk was seventy-something ex-college professor that had defeated old age by allowing young hippies and wanderers to take over his large house in a flat, farming valley along the Green River. He spent most of his days playing king of his castle, naked as the day he was born, debating life philosophies with the only other subset of the population that had the same amount of time he had for pondering big questions.

Since he had spent his entire career around the

college age set, he felt perfectly comfortable having them overrun his house, so comfortable in fact that he had long ago ceased to wear clothing of any sort, new comers who had a problem with that weren't the type he liked to hang around with anyway. At some point over the years, one of the guests had set little signs about such as "Wash Your Towels" and "You, Too, Can Buy Toilet Paper" so every new arrival could quickly get with the program and help out. The Echinacea fields surrounded the house on three sides and were managed by a red head named Chavez who wasted no time in getting Maya and Jesse two small hoes to remove weeds. As they walked over to their designated rows Maya whispered that "Chavez" was probably a Steinbeck fan too.

Jesse watched the sunset from the field, a glorious orange splash highlighting an already red-toned ridge above the valley. He hacked away at the little intruders sprouting up where they don't belong. After half an hour he was covered in dust as red as the sunset, it had found its way under his fingernails and inside his clothes, but he felt cleaner than he had ever felt in his life. This was living, this was life!

When the last bit of color had dipped below the horizon and the first stars twinkling their intent to transform the sky, Chavez walked over to the row where Jesse and Maya were bent over and told them they could finish up for the night. Jesse's back was already starting to twinge after less than two hours, how in the world do real farmers last all day? There was going to be a bonfire and he wanted their help carrying firewood.

He said they should stay two days, at least, because there was going to be a full moon rave out in the desert the next night and they could join him if they wanted to. The location was top secret and had just been released. The directions sounded crazy to Jesse. Once you got off the highway you were supposed to set your odometer to zero, go 4.2 miles, take a left onto a dirt road, reset your odometer for another 6.7 miles and so on. The chances that they would actually find the party sounded slim, but Jesse was game. Chavez was looking at Maya, of course, when he invited them, but it was Jesse who accepted. He'd heard about wild full moon raves, but had never been invited to one, of course Maya would be invited to this type of event without even trying.

"Let me tell you kids something about God," Hawk said, after taking a long inhale of his joint, the gray wisps mixing with the smoke from the fire. He reminded Jesse of an English teacher he had in high school (minus the nudity and weed). She had told Jesse's mom that he had potential. If only he would focus, or finish the homework, the teacher would transfer Jesse to the AP class and save him from the blue-collar cliff he was rapidly approaching.

"God doesn't exist." Hawk paused for dramatic effect, clearly enjoying the role of instigator or wise man, or maybe just pontificator. He was also clearly unaware that neither of his new audience members were religious. "There is no thing which can be named that is God. Is there a Great Unknown? Yes! Is there a What Is? Yes! This is truth. There is a 'What Is,' but you can't name it and you can't know it. Naming and knowing are processes that are contrary to the very nature of the 'What Is.' They are the process of defining. What does defining mean?" he asked.

Jesse wasn't sure if this was rhetorical so he waited a beat, but Maya jumped right in, her voice carrying strongly from the other side of the log circle. She had chosen to sit closer to Chavez than Jesse; Jesse hadn't said anything about wanting to get rid of her, but she definitely knew. "Defining? Like, to understand something?" she asked, sounding like the college student she was.

Jesse wanted to spend a moment understanding the situation he was in, defining *that*. Why was Maya all of a sudden so annoying? Why do women do that? Why do they act so perfect, and then reveal themselves after you have already made a commitment to them? Despite the current seating arrangement, he was obviously stuck on this road trip with her and he felt like he needed to figure out what it is he was doing with her, define the relationship in order to get a handle on this situation. But he was also interested in this old geezer's God ideas.

Hawk threw a handful of sage on the fire, causing a twittering of crackles and a warm, loving scent. "Defining means to outline what is the thing and what is not the thing. How do you know what something is? You know by what it is not. You draw a circle around a group of characteristics and christen that which is inside the circle with a name to distinguish it from that which is outside of the circle. That," he pointed, "is fire. We know it is fire and not water because we have defined that all things with fire characteristics are fire, while all things with water characteristics are water. Fire is fire, it is not water, and water is water, it can never be fire."

"And this is a woman," Chavez joked and put his arm around Maya, who didn't brush it off. Instead, she laughed.

Jesse felt a combined pang of annoyance that Maya was so literal and jealousy that Chavez was hitting on her. He wasn't confused about what Hawk was saying. He used names all the time to reduce unmanageable things in his life to manageable things. He even had a name for the feeling of being overwhelmed. Mr. Overwhelmed, or Maelstrom, as Jesse liked to call "him," came to visit the living room of Jesse's brain quite often. When he showed up, Jesse would do his best to greet him. He would think something like, "Oh hi, Maelstrom, so you're back. It's been a while, but I know you love to hang around when the restaurant is packed. So welcome, enjoy your stay, but please, try not to get underfoot. I'm really busy here." Jesse would imagine that, although Maelstrom had planned on taking over Jesse's brain in some hostile manner, causing chaos and panic to spread throughout

Jesse's body, once he was greeted properly, he just settled down in a corner somewhere and watched TV.

But what name could Jesse give for his feelings towards Maya? What name could he give for the thing that compelled him to take this road trip? Why did he leave his routine, his job, his friends, to go gallivanting across the country with this woman? For a moment he had thought that she could be his soulmate. That seemed farfetched now. He wasn't even sure he liked her all that much and she was sitting with another man's arm around her.

What about friends? Yes, Jesse could call them friends, except somehow that word didn't fit either. Ever since he first laid eyes on her, Jesse had a feeling that she was important. Certainly his life had gotten more interesting since he met her, even if it didn't feel improved at the moment. John would never have told Jesse about Hawk's farm if Maya hadn't been with him. He probably wouldn't have even picked Jesse up. So there were some benefits to this "thing" he and Maya had.

Chavez whispered something into Maya's ear that made her smile again. Jesse and Maya hadn't talked about being monogamous, but they *were* on a road trip together. Why wasn't Maya shoving that kid off her? Though, maybe he should be cool with this, Jesse reasoned. She wasn't his girlfriend. He didn't have a name for what she was to him, but seeing her all cozied up to another guy made him want to define their co-existence. If the relationship is not defined, the relationship is not under control. It could be anything. But if you call it a "monogamous relationship" you are distinguishing it from other interactions that are not monogamous relationships. And by the naming process, you are attempting to create a protective boundary around the thing, the relationship, a powerful boundary that will keep the evil spirits of lust or rejection away, some power and control over the natural instinct to fuck around.

"Wow! This campfire is getting hot," Chavez said, reaching behind him to pull his shirt off. It wasn't really that hot, Jesse noted. It was actually a cool night, sixty degrees probably. But Chavez had something to show off. The redhead was ripped. Removing his shirt revealed a broad, strong chest with not one but two gleaming golden nipple rings and a distinct six-pack with a seductive copper colored pleasure trail whispering it's way south.

"Heterosexual" was another one of those names Jesse couldn't help but acknowledge. Being a "heterosexual male," a much preferred title in Virginia, and probably everywhere else, was a name with a strong black border around it. "Heterosexuals males" only have sex with females and never, ever have sex with men. If you had sex with a man you were a "homosexual," another name, another black border. "Homosexuals" don't fall in love with women like Jesse does on a regular basis.

Of course there were "bisexuals," but even that term seemed restrictive. "Bisexual" sounds as if you must be an equal opportunist, yet Jesse's longings were toward specific people. He loved particular women and yet, although he had never hooked up with a man, he'd thought about it often enough. The term for people who currently fuck women, but would like to fuck men, is "bi-curious." Jesse hated the pejorative, condescending nature of that name. As if the person was young, still experimenting, and would soon settle down into a proper definition. Jesse was young, he knew, but he couldn't imagine that he would ever fit into one of those terms, not exactly. Yet, most adults do seem to settle into one definition or another. Did they wake up one day and just decide upon a permanent sexuality? Or do they spend their lives squeezing themselves into preexisting definitions that don't exactly fit?

Jesse had concluded in the past that the problem ceases to be an issue once you find your soulmate. But this time Jesse noticed that even thinking about his soulmate theory caused him to cringe, hopefully imperceptibly to the others. That was the very theory that got him into this situation.

His tendency to fall head over heels in love was starting to strongly resemble desperate grasping in the dark. As if all he needed was a soulmate and the emotional dark swirl around his sexual orientation would suddenly clear. Life would be filled with easy decisions; the forest would open up and reveal a single clear path upon which he'd skip along like Dorothy and her creatures. Now it dawned on him that he'd screwed it up, again. Instead of finding a soulmate, maybe he'd just grabbed ahold of the most soulmate-*like* person he could find, and the result was that he was deeper in the forest than ever, and jobless, and spending all of his savings, and sitting alone at a campfire with an old naked man and a couple that were starting to look like they were about to make an excuse and leave.

Soulmates, Jesse thought irritably, probably don't exist. It was just another word, another *name* we use to lasso up a bunch of characteristics, and the result is ungainly. This was what the old man was saying about God. The word wasn't the truth. The word, by its nature, is always less than the truth.

"So you're saying that to define something you must be able to distinguish between what it is and what it is not... and you can't do that with God because God is indistinguishable?" Jesse asked.

"Exactly!" Hawk said, hitting his wrinkled, naked thigh for emphasis, obviously pleased to have willing, young people to talk with about this.

"God, the name of the un-nameable," Maya said, sounding a little bored. Back at Safeway she was going to jump out of her skin with energy over politics, but now that they were talking about existential matters she was tuning out. How did Jesse end up traveling across the country with someone so polar opposite from him? And how did she end up on the polar opposite side of the bonfire?

"That is why when Moses asked God what his name was God did not say, 'How do you do, call me God the Almighty' he said, 'Yahweh,' which translates simply to I AM! God was telling Moses that there is no definition, no distinguishing between what or who God is, and what or who God is not. He said only, 'I am,' which is utterly indecipherable." Hawk glanced over and confused the resistance on Jesse's face for misunderstanding so he explained, "And this shows how truly powerful God is, right? If he had a name, then, by the very nature of names, he would be less than the All-Inclusive that we believe God to be. If he had a name then there would be something in this universe that was not God."

Jesse's resistance was this: Hawk was obviously very excited about God, but as he was talking Jesse realized that the problem Hawk described was not unique to the word "God." It was a problem with words in general. Can the small, four-letter word "bird" really hope to embody all that is *bird*? The magnificent white heron arching its wings at the river's edge *and* the small chickadee hopping deliberately from one branch to another? Language is simply ill-fitted clothing on things and ideas. We need it to communicate with each other, but we can't pretend that it is more than it is. We can't pretend that it is truth. Gay, straight, soulmate, bird—these words are simply the English language's attempt to encompass unwieldy truth.

Jesse spoke up, "But, Hawk, isn't that just the nature of language? It's impossible for a word to successfully encompass the essence of anything. Isn't that why language always evolves? Nothing quite fits perfectly, so people always feel compelled to come up with new words, especially for things that are important to us. Like how the Eskimos ended up with over twenty different words for 'snow.'"

"And Americans have at least that many for money, fucking greedy bastards," Chavez said. Jesse wanted to comment that renaming yourself "Chavez" and growing Echinacea on some hippy's ranch didn't completely distinguish you from being an American, but Maya spoke first.

"They are called Inuit," Maya interjected. "Eskimo is considered pejorative."

"My point is that when something is important, people are compelled to keep trying to find a name that feels right, that fits. There is a compulsion to hold, with a name, the thing you adore. But finding a sufficient name is impossible, words are always imperfect," Jesse said.

"Names are by their nature reductionary," Hawk went on. "The Jews won't say or write the name of God because it is a power grab, and they know it. To honor God, you don't attempt to name him. But it isn't just the Jews who believe in the power of names. History is full of stories about the power of names. Elders caution their children about this power through stories. Take Rumpelstiltskin, for example. That is a story, by the way, that appears in so many different cultures it is considered by folklorists to be one of the story archetypes. From South America to Croatia there are Rumpelstiltskin-type children's stories where knowing someone's true name takes away their power."

"Why do we say 'God' in English instead of saying "Yahweh," or some other English word that means 'I am who I am'?" Or is that what the word 'God' means?" Maya asked. Of course she would be more interested in etymology than fairytales. The girl was getting more bland by the minute, Jesse couldn't help but think; but he had to stop being so negative. He looked up at the bright moon, it was almost full and had been outshining the stars' attempts to stake their claim on the night sky.

"No, no. God is from a proto-Indo-European word that means 'to invoke' or 'to call.' It is a way to call the Supreme Being to you and, again, it's a power grab. How do you, a tiny, insignificant monkey in this enormous universe, gain the power to force God to pay attention to you? To be concerned with your problems? You use a name. A name that has the power to call forth this greatness to you. The first use of the word 'God' was in early Christian literature, but Christians weren't the first people in history to attempt to use a name to invoke the power of the universe to benefit themselves. People in different cultures have done this from time immemorial, and to the extent that it worked for them they continued, and felt powerful. Christians, for example, have had a decent run of things for the past 2,000 years, and they interpret this to mean that they have pull with God, a power to sway this great force that they are comfortable naming and calling upon for even the smallest of daily favors.

"But, if you listen to very spiritual people, you will quickly find that the more spiritual a person is the more agnostic he becomes. You realize that you, a small being, cannot hope to fully understand, define, and then leash the power of the Almighty. Even Pope Benedict said agnostics, who really struggle with the question of God, are closer to the Kingdom of God than supposed believers who simply go to church as part of their routine. They know something great is there, but cannot expect to understand its full nature, and therefore do not presume to define or name what it is. On the other hand, people trying to make power grabs, concerned with lots of material things—televangelists are the best example—use the name God so frequently you'd assume it was their personal dishrag. Truly spiritual people do not so easily violate the third commandment and take his name in vain."

It occurred to Jesse that Hawk was using the name quite liberally. For ease of the conversation, of course, but wasn't that the usual, benign, purpose of using the word? He decided to jump in. "Names aren't just for invoking power though, they assist with communication. Without communication we are unable to connect with each other. How would this conversation have gone if you had never allowed yourself to use the word 'God'?"

"I think what Hawk is trying to say is that using the name God to invoke God to do your wishes is wrong, not just using the name to have a conversation," Maya said. Jesse wondered if she was purposefully avoiding looking at the deeper meaning, despite her fancy college education, or maybe because of it.

"Maya, he is saying that the very act of naming is the sin, no matter the context," Jesse said, a little too curtly. He looked at her and she looked right back at him. The tension in the air between them could have fueled a bonfire on its own. Jesse realized that Maya was wearing Chavez as a shield.

"You know, there is no getting away from hearing people say 'God'" Hawk interjected, ignoring their quibble, "and I've come to enjoy it. I like to think of it not as a noun, but a verb. Like I said before—it means to invoke, or to call. But instead of thinking of it as bringing the Almighty's grace upon myself, I like to think of it as bringing myself to the Almighty. Like a Tibetan bell reminding its listeners to return to focused meditation, the word "God" is sprinkled throughout my day in the media and conversations. I choose to use it as a reminder to take a breath and feel the joy and gratitude that comes so naturally when you return to your highest self."

"I guess I'm an agnostic," Jesse offered. "I'm not a great spiritual seeker, but I can't say I know the truth of the matter either way." Actually, agnosticism was his current state of being with everything, he thought. "It's more due to the fact that I can't stick with a decision to save my life!" he joked. Hawk chuckled, but Maya didn't.

"Well, decision making has never been an issue

for me. It's easy to see which way to go when you have your feet planted in reality. I'm an atheist. When you die there is no la la land or singing fairies. The worms eat you and that's it. Kaput. End of story," Maya said, looking at Jesse when she said 'kaput.' She looked annoyed. Maybe she was right to be annoyed. It was Jesse who threw her up on the pedestal that might not fit; Jesse who concocted this fantasy of sailing across the country on a wave of love to meet a child.

"How can you be so certain?" Chavez asked Maya.

"Maya is certain about everything, from PC terminology to the most intangible matters, just try her, any topic—she's certain!" Jesse said, keeping his voice light and fun. Maya smiled at Jesse. Had he invented the tension he'd been feeling for the last hour or so in his head? Did he make up the love glow, too? Was everything in his head? Maybe she was on this trip not for him, but for her own reasons, and it didn't matter to her if they fought. Maybe he was the only one that would fall if the bubble burst. He looked over at Hawk, who seemed to be temporarily stunned by Maya's atheist comment.

"To each his own," Hawk finally said, a tad wistfully. He was done with his lecture now that he was dealing with real people with their own theories instead of empty vessels to fill with his. "To each his own." He repeated softly.

They watched the flames flicker against the sweet valley air. The feeling he was having, Jesse finally decided, was confusion. He had been feeling this way, he recognized now, ever since that night in the club. He had interpreted the feeling as love. Love, real love, he could only guess must feel like confusion. At least a little. But confusion wasn't love in the same way that stomach flu wasn't love (even if both things give you a fluttery feeling in your belly when they first come on). Confusion was just what it was.

Hello, confusion, come on in and have a drink, the lounge in Jesse's brain accepts all kinds. We'll name you Charlie.

CHAPTER THIRTEEN

MAYA WAS LAYING on a rock, her black hair, damp from the sweat of dancing, was spilling over the edge of the rock like a waterfall, and her creamy skin was glowing in the bright moonlight. Jesse admired her beauty, her curves, and the confident way she seemed to be draping her body so seductively, the rock serving as her showcase, for her own enjoyment, without regard to whether or not he or anyone else was watching. He had lost sight of her a few hours earlier when they had gotten separated. When he had gone away from the main encampment to look for a place to shit. There didn't seem to be any porta potties around, which was really gross because there is no way he was the only one that usually had to take a dump when he started coming on to uppers, so he'd had to wander way out into the desert and dig a little hole. By the time he came back Maya had been grabbed up by Chavez and was dancing in the crowd. Jesse had wandered over to the food and booze table and gotten sucked into a conversation about the different textures of clothing they were all wearing. One girl had an especially soft fur trim on her jacket that everyone was taking turns petting.

While he was high he hadn't minded the fact that Maya and Chavez were off doing who know what out of his sight. He'd reasoned that maybe the excitement, the thrill he felt for Maya wasn't excitement or thrill for love, but for the gateway she represented. Gateway to what? To adventure? To self? Maybe the great love story of this road trip wasn't a girl, but the trip itself. He just needed space from his identity as Jesse of Adam's Morgan to really figure out what he wanted from his life, who he was. He didn't need a soulmate, he needed an uncomfortable road trip! He'd yelled into the crowd, "I'm on an uncomfortable road trip!" and several people hooted and applauded.

Despite his acceptance of his situation, Jesse felt great relief when he happened upon Maya, alone. She was obviously still pretty high too, she looked so relaxed on that rock, Jesse thought that maybe this was a good moment to talk how traveling with someone intensifies a relationship; speeds things along. It wasn't their fault that they had fallen in love, had mad passionate sex, had their first squabble, and gotten bored already. Maybe if they talked they could have a meeting of minds. And, sex.

Jesse looked around. There were only a few stragglers still dancing to the thump, bump of the techno music. For most of the night there had been forty or fifty people pulsing their bodies under the full moonlight, but dawn was now threatening, and most of the revelers had crawled off to a tent or their cars. Chavez, thankfully, had disappeared.

"Hey, are you hungry? Let's get out of here and find a motel near a restaurant now—crash out for a day. We don't have to be in Santa Cruz until, what, Thursday? We have a ton of time. Maybe I can help you feel like you belong." He said, alluding to her stated desires and his. Jesse stared at the eastern horizon, where the sun was brightening the sky, hoping his awkward innuendo worked. But before she could answer, her telephone rang. Watching the sunrise after dancing all night at a rave is the right moment to reconnect with your traveling partner, not to answer your phone, Jesse though irritably. But she did, and she was quickly waist-deep in a conversation with some sobbing girlfriend who, from what Jesse gathered, was just dumped on her ass. She was on the telephone so long that Jesse leaned back against the rock and started to drift off to sleep.

"Jesse! Don't you agree?" Maya's voice woke Jesse, who suddenly felt very sober and very achy. The rock was definitely not as comfortable as it was a half-hour before, and the heat they felt from dancing was gone. It was cold. "I mean, it's just the facts, right? Women have to put men in two categories." Maya had extracted herself from her friend's emotional crisis and seemed to assume that Jesse was listening to the conversation. "Either men are for fun or for real, and the minute they are not for real they are out of that category."

"What is the 'for real' category?" Jesse hesitated to ask. He stood up and stretched. They definitely needed to get going to a hotel. He pulled her off the rock and they started walking to the car.

"It's marriage, kids, the whole shebang."

"So you're saying that it's either marriage or nothing? How old-fashioned! What about a healthy monogamous relationship?"

"I'm for monogamy by choice. The point of marriage is that you are declaring that you accept no longer having a choice about monogamy—you're willing to give up the choice for the other benefits," she said.

Jesse opened the car door for Maya. "Sheesh, how romantic of you. You make it sound like a business relationship." He went over to the driver's side. The car felt warm and cozy, the seat cushion almost luxurious. Jesse realized that he was dead tired and on the brink of a long hangover. Instead of starting the car he leaned the seat back. Maya did the same, and then curled her body sideways to face him.

"Look, my cousin lived with a man for seven years, *seven years*, before she realized that the fact that they never got married was because he never wanted to marry her. She wasted so much time believing all of his new-age crap about how marriage promotes a system of patriarchy, overpopulation, was bad for the planet, and blah, blah, blah.... but you know what? After they broke up he met another woman and was married with a baby, within two years. If a man doesn't want to get married to you he doesn't want to get married to *you*. If you use marriage for what it is: a 'shit or get off the pot' tool, you won't waste your time being monogamous with some prick that isn't really deeply in love with you."

"Wow, sourpuss! One bad story shouldn't undermine trust. Lots of couples live happy, monogamous lives without getting married." Not that Jesse knew many of them personally, but, for once, he felt like arguing. Something about being back in the car was giving him a king in his own castle feeling.

"You mean serial monogamy. Like I said, I'm all for not fucking anyone else if you aren't in the mood to fuck anyone else." Maya liked to swear when she was making a point, Jesse noted.

"So you're saying that you refuse to be monogamous, to promise monogamy, before you are married?"

"If people followed this simple path there would be way less heartbreak in the world," Maya declared.

And then there was silence. Even if Jesse was still into her, and he had all but decided that he wasn't, this type of conversation wasn't supposed to happen so early in their relationship. They had only known each other a couple of weeks. The acceleration of a relationship is the curse and the joy of road trips, he thought again. He was not planning on being monogamous with Maya, but her blatant declaration that she was going to have sex with other men—that was what she was saying, right? —was a turn-off and smacked of an admission about what might have happened with Chavez earlier. Jesse didn't want to know about what happened with Chavez. It was time to lighten the mood.

"So, I guess that means that mean we're not stopping at a drive-through chapel in Las Vegas?" he joked, but Maya didn't respond. She was staring out the window. The car filled with silence again as it went from cozy to claustrophobic.

What they really needed to do to turn this day around, Jesse decided, was to get going and have sex somewhere. He popped his seat back up and turned on the car.

"I feel awkward. I guess I thought I already told you my monogamy theories back at Splendex..." Maya finally breached the silence, raising her seat too.

Jesse pulled out of the parked line of cars, heading back along the dirt road. He checked his dashboard to make sure he still had the directions, then clicked his odometer to zero, 5.7 miles to the turn off, then right, then 3.2 miles... "No, it's cool. You're probably right anyway. I just..." Jesse struggled to find the right thing to say.

"You just couldn't deal with an open relationship," she finished for him.

"No, I don't think so. Not that I'm not willing to try!" he added, as a last grasp on any chance of sex that day. He looked over at her with a big fake grin and saw that she wasn't convinced, so he gave in to honesty. "Look, truthfully, we're too young to think about marriage. But the idea of an open relationship kills the romance."

"And it's all about romance and sugar plum fantasies for you?"

"Well, yeah, I wouldn't have called it that, but the romance is part of the game. It's a turn-on." This was such bullshit that he was not even convincing himself. Jesse knew he was not romantic. Past girlfriends had specifically told him that he was lacking in that area. But Maya didn't mean flowers and chocolates. She was talking about beer goggles, mood lighting, and red silk panties. The swirl of fantasy that comes crashing down when the woman who rocked your world last night gets up in the morning, puts on stained, grannie underwear, and then tries to kiss you with morning breath. "I guess I'm just a dreamer. Hard to find men like me these days." He smiled, not knowing why he was even trying to sell himself to her since he already decided he was going to dump her the first chance he got. Just instinct, probably (plus, he was still hoping to get laid).

"No, sorry to burst your bubble, but most men are exactly like that. You guys are all about putting a woman up on a pedestal and surrounding her with some big fantasy until the day comes when she farts, or acts insecure, or some real human thing that suddenly catapults her real human self into the guy's awareness. And his reaction is to assume, not that his fantasy is impossible, but rather that he had mistakenly identified this particular girl or that she has 'changed' and then he cheats or drops her in his quest to find the real fantasy girl."

"Wow, sounds like you've been through it. What happened?" He geared up his sensitive listening voice. Maya's anger was palatable and, although it made her even less attractive to him, Jesse was intrigued at her accurate summation of most every relationship he had ever had. He felt curious about her experience. The woman's perspective. Or at least he might as well pass the time with conversation, since they obviously weren't looking for a private pull out somewhere.

"Oh, it was this guy Steve at college. He is a ceramics artist. If you've ever dated someone who can throw pots, you know about the power of those hands. Steve could hold me... sculpt me...well...I was putty in his hands." Maya smirked at her own pun. Jesse relaxed a little. If she was willing to show still raw feelings about an ex-boyfriend, Jesse figured it was her way of acknowledging the thing that was too awkward to say—the magic was gone between them, but perhaps a friendship was still hanging on. Maybe friends with benefits, Jesse hoped.

"Ceramic artist, huh? I should try one of those. So

far my experience with artists hasn't been so great. My last girlfriend went to the Corcoran College of Art and cheated on me with some painter." Not that he'd been perfectly faithful to her, but Maya didn't need all the details, even if they were now officially girlfriend gabbing about exes.

"Well, Steve was into my open relationship idea, but neither of us was interested in anyone else for about six months, until my roommate and I decided to stop shaving. Then suddenly he said that he needed to go on this spirit walk with a blond pianist."

"Oh, come on! You can't blame a man for choosing blond hottie musician over hairballs."

"But the hairballs were real! That is my point. When real shows up, the men leave."

"I think you're being unfair, and I happen to have first-hand knowledge that you're fairly hairless these days," he teased, but inside he was grossed out by the image of her covered in hair. There was no way he'd deal with that. Plus, she had to be so serious all the time. Why slap down every joke he tried to make? What happened to the cute, flirtatious girl he'd met at the club just two weeks ago?

"Well, my hairy phase didn't last long. My feminist principles were secondary to my sex life." She laughed, finally.

"Speaking of sex life, I don't think I can drive all of the way to that hot spring you wanted to hit today. Let's find a motel." Is there something wrong with me? Jesse thought, that I am trying for sex when even *I'm* not into it? Looking back at his life, though, he had to admit that it would be difficult to find a situation where he'd walked away from an opportunity to have sex and, despite the problems, there was an opportunity to have sex today.

"You still want to have sex after that conversation? Wow. I was thinking that we were slipping into friend mode...."

"I guess we are, huh," Jesse admitted. He almost added "friends with benefits" but, actually, Maya being so straightforward was a relief.

"It's just that, and I hope this doesn't upset you, because I really like you, but I've been thinking about this as we've been traveling and...I could never get totally serious with someone who isn't 100 percent straight," Maya said.

Jesse almost fell through the bottom of the car under the weight of that lead ball.

"What! You think I'm gay just because you met me in a gay club?" Anger welled up inside Jesse. She was wrong. He loved fucking women. He'd been fucking her all week whenever he had the chance. But, if he was totally honest, he thought, he'd love fucking men, too. It was just that it hadn't happened for him yet. Not that it couldn't happen. He'd had a ton of guys try flirting with him—but he turned them down. Not because he didn't want to, more because the intensity of it all scared him. With a woman he felt like he was in control of himself and the situation at hand. Even if she was on top, he never lost his power, his control. With a man, who knew what would happen. He might dissolve.

"No! It has nothing to do with the club. I don't know, maybe it was the club. Maybe my gaydar is out of whack. I didn't mean to offend you or anything. Being gay is totally normal for, like, 10 percent of the population you know." She was back peddling. "I just, um, at first thought you were one of those gay guys that likes to fuck women. Then, when you invited me on this trip, I thought maybe you were bi."

"Wait, back up. How many gay guys do you know who like to fuck women?" Jesse fumed. He may be a kid from the suburbs, but he had spent years in the party scene, and there were some things he thought he had a grip on, like the fucking definition of gay.

"I grew up in California, Jesse. I've met all the flavors. Gay men that like the occasional soft feel of a woman. Straight men who take advantage of the quick and easy gay lay. Omnivores who will fuck anything that bats an eyelash at them. It isn't a big deal. People do what they like." She said it so casually Jesse believed her instantly. He'd thought he was big stuff moving from Reston, Virginia to Adam's Morgan, the party capital of Washington DC, Mr. Seen-It-All working behind the bar in a big city—and suddenly he felt like he hadn't seen so much.

He let the word "omnivore" roll around in his mouth. Now there was a title, a name, that could fit him. An "omnivore" sounded much more liberating than "bi-sexual." An omnivore ate what it pleased, when it pleased, and wasn't tied down by some pre-determined rule about who it should want to fuck in the moment.

"But isn't everyone an omnivore deep inside?" Jesse cringed. Did he just say that out loud?

"I'm not, Jesse. The one time I made out with a girl I spent the entire time wishing she had a penis so we could actually get somewhere. I think if you draw a line where 0 is straight and 100 is gay, most of us are way over to one side or the other. Like an inverse bell curve. I don't know where you are on the spectrum. I'm way over by the 0, probably around 8 or 10 because I can appreciate a woman's figure, but I can't imagine touching a vag, and I know I couldn't be in a relationship with a woman. It would feel way too unbalanced for me. And plus, like I said, there would be no penis." Maya might have continued talking about penises or her uneventful lesbian love moments, but Jesse was only half-listening. The word "omnivore" was ringing too loudly in his ears. How had he managed to not make any omnivore friends? He lived right near DuPont Circle, the gay neighborhood of DC, but somehow he hadn't met anyone in the middle of this gay-straight spectrum. There were two gay guys in his theater group, but they were the limp-wrist Andy Warhol type of gay. Definitely gay, gay. Not having sex with women gay.

Jesse felt frustrated. He had specifically sought out an interesting group of people to run with after he'd made his big transition to the city. Artist/waitress girlfriend (for a few months anyway), one buddy in a rock cover band, another buddy who was a bike courier tattooed from head to toe. And that night at Splendex wasn't his first time at a gay club, either. His friend, Slaven, had figured out about fag hags, and they started going months ago. They thought it was hilarious to dress up androgynously, take drugs, and seek out the few women in the crowd. Was that the telltale sign of a sexual omnivore? Was he brave enough to ask Slaven? And, he had never said this out loud, but how many times had he jerked off to the image of being slammed from behind by some big leather "bear"? It hadn't occurred to him that the fantasy could be a reality. Way too scary. Not for him. Could he really do that? Just the thought made him feel a little repulsed, and his cock swelled. Holy fuck! Jesse thought, maybe I am bisexual? Or something. Anyway, one thing was certain, he had to get out of this car and go forth into the world with this new thought. They had to get to California ASAP.

"California, the land of opportunity, huh? Let's keep driving then. I'm wide awake. Let's drive through the night," Jesse said as casually as he could.

"Whatever you say, Romeo" she laughed. Maya was cool enough not to make Jesse admit what they both knew he was thinking. In fact, Jesse decided, again, Maya was pretty cool altogether. He could totally see her as his wing-woman at some fantastic

San Francisco club.

"I think this is the beginning of a beautiful friendship," Jesse said, and reached over to punch Maya's shoulder.

"Me too, Jesse." She smiled and punched him back.

CHAPTER FOURTEEN

THE PLAN WAS to labor at home as long as possible. Gyrate her body to the early contractions in her own warm nest with her loving husband at her side. They had chicken soup in case she grew hungry, and her favorite Creamsicle in the freezer. Marvin had a whole lineup of relaxing new age music from the yoga studio. They were going to flow and sway and chant. They were also going to have sex. Having sex in early labor was supposed to loosen the cervix and, since Jean was determined to do a natural birth, she wanted her cervix wide open. Of course, none of that happened.

Around midnight, two weeks before the due date, just as Marvin and Jean were headed to bed after a marathon of old episodes of 24, she went to pee and a huge, bloody clod dropped out of her. She called the on-call midwife (who was one of five midwifes that might attend her labor, depending on who was on duty when she popped) who informed her that losing this "mucus plug" meant that she was going to have her baby in either two hours, or two weeks. Sort of like the old joke about cold medicine reducing the duration of a cold from a week to seven days.

She'd grown accustomed to the Braxton-Hicks contractions, the little ones that weren't supposed to mean anything, every few hours for over a month; but after losing the mucus plug, she became hyper aware of the periodic tightening in her belly. At the very next squeeze she told Marvin that they should probably go in to the hospital, just in case. He gently reminded her that their plan was to wait until the contractions were so strong she had to stop moving in order to endure them. Feeling another, slightly stronger contraction, she told him that she'd changed her mind, and he should call his mother right away to come over and stay with Sienna.

Marvin tried again. "Honey, it's past midnight. My mother is sound asleep, and you heard the midwife; losing your plug, or whatever it's called, doesn't mean that you are going into labor. Let's try to get some sleep, and if you're still feeling the contractions in the morning, we can go in and have it checked out." Checked out, he said, like Jean was a carburetor.

Jean's loving husband didn't seem so loving now that the labor might interfere with his sleep, she thought angrily. She looked around and realized that nothing else was right, either. Behind her selfish husband was a couch with the pillows all messed up. Why couldn't they arrange the pillows after they got up each time?

Jean went to arrange the pillows, but facing the couch gave her a view of the kitchen, where she saw a much larger problem. The dishes were done (they had an arrangement that every night one of them was in charge of bedtime with Sienna while the other person did dishes), except for the little plates and spoons from dessert (they routinely snuck sweets after Sienna was asleep). But the various appliances were a disaster! The coffee maker was at an odd angle to the toaster, and the blender was in several pieces piled around the counter. Jean rushed over to adjust the offending appliances into straight lines, but upon closer inspection, things went from bad to worse, because now she could see that each of them were filthy. And a mismatch of color. What kind of haphazard family had a white toaster, a black coffee maker, and a stainless steel blender? Jean turned to complain to Marvin but he had retreated upstairs to the bedroom (the nerve!). She looked at the clock again; Macy's was definitely not open at this hour, so there was nothing she could do about the colors. But she could certainly clean these things.

Marvin came back downstairs and found Jean scrubbing away at the appliances in the sink. "It is one thirty in the morning, sweetie. Let's go to bed,

and I'll help you wash these things in the morning,"
he said gingerly, like every word from his lips shook
a carbonated beverage that might explode all over
him.

This was their third child, but his first pregnancy.
When they were teenagers, their love fell to fear
fairly quickly after Jean got pregnant, and their
mothers decided to save the young marriage by
keeping them in separate houses until after the baby
was born (after which, their freshly minted family
moved into the room over the garage at Jean's
parents' house). So Jean had fun walks in the park
with her "husband," and then went home so her
mother could hold her hair while she puked in the
toilet. When the big date arrived she was in the
delivery room with her mother, and Marvin hung
out in the lobby with his. So Marvin was sailing
uncharted waters tonight and, it dawned on Jean
suddenly, perhaps he was not the best person in the
world to labor alone with.

Jean didn't feel like such an expert at this herself.
Birthing a baby at seventeen was a different thing
entirely than doing it at thirty-eight. For one thing,
although the natural movement was well known in
California in the nineties, Jean's mother made sure
her precious (if not pure) daughter was pumped full
of every pain-killing drug available when she had
Maverick. The main thing she remembers was that
the hospital room, her first, was much more gritty
than they look in the movies. She expected a pristine
white room with big bouquets of flowers. But the

room was about as pristine as its occupant, both of them with their virginity quite obviously lost. Marvin had bought her a bouquet from the hospital store, which her mother placed next to the after-delivery bed. It had daises and roses and a little plastic teddy bear with some soft fuzzy stuff painted on it. Later, after she broke off the long stick at the bottom and gave it to baby Maverick, he sucked that fuzz off its ears. At seventeen, Jean wasn't very knowledgeable about the hazards of toxic toys for babies.

The pregnancy had been so different, too. When Jean was seventeen, her main concern was looking fat, which she didn't. Jean had photos. Seventeen-year-olds (at least the ones pre-obesity epidemic) look just exactly how a movie star was supposed to look pregnant: thin and glowing, with the cutest baby-bump sitting primly on the front. Now more than twice (twice!) the age she was with the first baby, her body had decided to multiply the baby bumps as well. The two that took over her butt cheeks showed up a good month before any evidence of pregnancy showed itself on her front side. Then the bumps kept coming: two watermelons appeared where her boobs were previously located, and then merged with her growing belly so thoroughly that, by the end, it looked as though her belly had Mickey Mouse ears.

During her second trimester, she was running after Sienna at the playground and pulled the relaxed ligaments in her hips, causing such excruciating pain that she had to use a cane for weeks just to hobble around. Her hair did grow thick and luxurious, except this time the early gray strands that had eagerly sprung through the gates the moment she turned thirty, like they had been waiting impatiently for years, decided to join in the fun and birth their own babies. And because she was determined to give this baby the ideal, perfect start that her other two children, both birthed by teen moms, never got, she had gone without hair color for the duration. So, about two inches of gray roots crowned her fat, limping, glorious pregnant self.

But she was happy. It was actually the first time in her life that she didn't care how she looked. She felt like she had gained superpowers that obfuscated the trivial concerns of normal people. Marvin helped with the initial spark, of course, but she was singlehandedly making eyeballs, and toes, and all the major organs needed for life. Like Einstein, she was way too important to worry about having perfect hair.

"I need to go to the hospital," Jean told Marvin, who was standing there half-asleep, staring at her. "I'm having a ton of contractions, I can't go to sleep, and I don't want to do this alone." She almost added a sarcastic, "I'm sorry it's not a convenient time for you," but she held her tongue. She didn't want her baby to come into this world in the middle of a marital squabble, even if her husband deserved it.

Marvin walked over and hugged her. "Oh, babe. You're not alone. I am right here. If it's okay with you, I'll make some coffee with this shiny clean coffee maker." Jean looked at him. Was he really considering messing up her hard work? "You know, I bet there will be some at the hospital," he revised, and went to pack an overnight bag. After he put the bag and a half-asleep Sienna in the car, he came back into the house and said, "I'm sorry, Jean, I guess I'm just in a little shock. I had my mind set that we had two more weeks and, I guess I didn't feel ready yet...but don't worry. I'm here for you. I'm ready now." He took her hand, led her to the coat closet, and held up her favorite blue Patagonia jacket.

"You don't feel ready? What about me?! I still have to finish that lease agreement for Aramho, Inc. God, why didn't I hire an assistant?" Jean asked. Way too late, she tried to think if Maverick came early too, but she couldn't remember. She remembers not knowing exactly when she got pregnant with Maverick, but there must have been a sonogram, right? Important little details that just disappeared into the abyss of motherhood.

Then a contraction hit her so hard she couldn't stand up under the weight of it. Marvin caught her and they breathed through it together. Wynn had advised Jean to breathe "hee, hee" so that she kept pressure on her cervix with every breath. Wynn said it helped her get her second baby out in record time. It wasn't about surviving the contractions, she said, it was about using them. But pushing the baby out wasn't Jean's goal at the moment. This baby was coming too soon! Thinking about all of her unfinished work, Jean started to panic. "Maybe I should go into my office and try to finish a few things right now," she said. This time Marvin looked at her like she was crazy.

"Aramho is going to have to wait, sweetie. Let's get you into this jacket." Marvin only called Jean sweetie when he was feeling frustrated with her. Why is he frustrated with me? She thought. I'm the one having the baby! Jean put the jacket on. On the way to the car she had another contraction. Marvin checked his watch, but didn't say anything. He didn't have to. This baby was coming. Ready or not.

"I wonder if it's all this stress over Maya that brought on the early labor," Jean said to Marvin as they drove through the dark streets of their neighborhood. "I've probably freaked my poor little baby out with all the stress hormones I've had lately. Maybe he wants out of me just to be done with it."

"I'm sure it doesn't have anything to do with that. He is just ready to meet his family, Jean, that's all. Some come a little early, some come a little late. It's totally normal," Marvin replied. Like most men, Marvin was biologically incapable of understanding the self-blame that women traditionally lather upon themselves.

When they arrived at the hospital, Jean was only two centimeters dilated. Marvin, who had already woken his mother up, restrained himself from saying, "I told you so." Normally the hospital would send them back home because they couldn't admit mothers who were less than four centimeters, but the maternity ward was surprisingly empty and they were allowed to stay.

Jean climbed up on the bed and did the "hee, hee" breathing for the next couple of contractions with her legs pulled up and spread like she was already having the baby. She could feel the pressure on her cervix when she did a strong "hee" exhale, so maybe Wynn was right. Marvin busied himself by setting up their little Bluetooth speaker system, but Jean couldn't imagine even noticing music right now. What was it with men and electronics? After he had it playing, though, she enjoyed it. Marvin was a good man. She was happy that he was there. Thank goodness he was there, because she felt like she was on a roller coaster and everything was spinning out of control. She wished they had brought Sienna here instead of dropping her off at Grandma's. The baby wasn't here yet, and already it was causing Sienna to be separated from her mother during such a big important family moment. Jean considered asking Marvin to go get her, but a huge wave of pain flooded her body before she could speak. Then, due to the magic of labor, the pain receded and was gone again, as if it didn't exist at all.

Somewhere along the way (maybe at Sienna's birth?) a midwife told Jean that there was a flood of endorphins with each contraction, and in this slow way a laboring woman's pain tolerance builds along with the intensity of the labor. It was a just a casual comment, without reference to any real scientific studies, but Jean remembered it, and was relying on it. Maybe it would have happened with her first baby, if she hadn't been so medicated.

Jean's endorphins didn't have time to catch up in this birth. The whole thing took less than six hours and, toward the end, the contractions were so intense she seriously regretted going the natural route. In addition to the racking, pure pain, in between each contraction she felt either freezing cold or burning hot. The nurse did attempt to give her something to "take the edge off," at the last minute, but the baby came screaming out like hot lightning on the very next contraction so it was too little, too late. The birth, Jean decided later when she had a moment to think about it, was all about Arvin, her body simply acting as an extension of his will. Unlike the concentrated pushing she remembered from Maverick's birth, Arvin moved out of her body on an expedited schedule, and it was all she could do to just get out of his way. Her emotions, her body, her mind, all of her had to move out of his way. So, instead of trying to remember the words to one of Marvin's yogi chants, she threw her head back and screamed herself backwards while Arvin came forward into the world.

In a meditation class at the Divine Center, Jean had been told to focus on her breathing and, when she noticed that she was distracted by "monkey brain" jibber-jabber, she must refocus on her breathing. It was very hard to do. But, supposedly, if you spend a lot of time practicing, you will be rewarded with an experience: a feeling of no-self.

Jean had never achieved this through mediation. But now she knew what it was, because she felt it in labor. The birthing experience, she decided, gives women a leg up on becoming spiritually enlightened beings.

After Maverick was born, Jean kept hearing this voice in her head: "The Age of Jean is over! Long live Maverick!" It didn't upset her too much, because she was so in love with him, and, thank goodness, it turned out not to be true. Jean had had a very full life over the years. Until now, she had forgotten that she felt that way those first few days so long ago. But, after Arvin's birth, Jean felt the same way again. Long live Arvin! And she knew, beyond a doubt, that she wasn't the only mother who'd had that feeling after giving birth to a baby. It must be common.

But what about women who give up their babies for adoption? They still felt what it was like to be set aside for another life. They still went through pregnancy and labor. Yet they knew "their" time would continue to be for them, unless they had other children. All of these years Jean just assumed, hoped maybe, that Maya didn't have the same intense experience of being set aside for a child. She was so young, Jean thought, maybe Maya would just move on with her life as if nothing ever happened. But her labor with Arvin quashed any hope of that. There was no forgetting or moving on from having a baby. It was impossible. Even if you never regret your decision to give a baby up for adoption, even if you remain satisfied that it was the best decision for everyone involved, in some way the Age of You is affected. The Age of Before is dead. Of course Maya had come knocking. What a fool she was to expect otherwise.

CHAPTER FIFTEEN

IT WAS TWO in the morning, and Jesse only had fifty miles to go, now forty-nine. He remembered some advertisement about a fancy sedan that would effuse lemon-scented oil or something at you if its sensors notice that your eyes were drooping. Does that shit really work? Does it spray out of the visor? Was it a light mist? Maybe a cool one? Real lemon, or just a scent like those plug-in scents Aunt Jessica uses? Didn't it come out that that stuff was toxic? Pine fresh going straight to your thyroid? Rich people have personal doctors to warn them about that health stuff, Jesse thought, a Bentley would have some sort of natural essential oil. Pure lemon zest for the wealthy, artificial cancer stink for the peons.

Even fake lemon would probably still help you wake up though, Jesse thought. He had to keep shaking himself to keep his body active and stay awake. He'd open the window and get a little fresh air on his face, but Maya was sleeping sweetly next to him. He didn't want to wake her up with wind. He looked over and noticed she had put the seat back so far she was almost lying flat. Her seat belt was off and seeing that caused a shiver of stress in his chest. Once in high school a friend of Jesse's went right through his windshield because he wasn't wearing a seat belt when he crashed. His belted passenger was fine.

I won't fall asleep though, Jesse thought. He never fell asleep watching TV, or movies, or driving. Sleeping wasn't easy for Jesse. He couldn't have music playing, and it drove him crazy to have even a tiny night light on. He didn't know how other people could deal with that distraction. For Jesse, sleep was a prize not to be taken for granted. Like taking acid, Jesse was liable to end up with hours of teeth-grinding panic if he didn't have the proper set and setting. Body relaxed, mind quiet, lights out, silent.

But he was a little too relaxed now. They had driven straight from the full moon, all-night rave to a natural hot spring in the desert Maya knew about. Jesse tried to nap in the car when they arrived, but the late-morning sun made it uncomfortably hot, so he had only slept for about an hour before giving up and wandering in the direction Maya had gone earlier.

Jesse followed a narrow dirt path down a barren

hill. He couldn't remember what Maya had said about how far it was. A few minutes, or a few miles? After about ten minutes, he got the feeling that he was totally alone in the desert. All around him there was nothing but burnt orange rocks and tufts of uncomfortable-looking grass. Here and there he spotted a few angry bushes that looked like they wanted to tumble off and find their fortunes elsewhere. But the sky was an amazing, thick, endless blue, with white, puffy clouds leisurely floating about. And, after trying for an hour to sleep curled up in a car seat, stretching his body with the movement of walking felt good, freeing even. Soon enough, the pungent smell of sulfur let Jesse know he was on the right path after all. When he walked around the bend he was somewhat shocked. He had walked out of the desert into a full-on oasis.

The hot spring rested ahead of him on a small hill. The source itself was a large brown mound formed by mineral precipitating from the hot spring and algae living off the hot water. The water flowed downhill from the mound to nurture green grasses and reeds. There were a couple of cows standing about eating the grass. Someone had hauled enough cement out here to form a catchment system leading to a small pool, with the overflow into a larger one below it. The cows weren't the only beings that had found this bit of paradise in the desert. Having just spent the last half-hour totally, completely alone in the desert, Jesse couldn't help but notice that there were a surprising number of humans stuffed into the pools. Fifteen people, all as naked as the day they were born.

It was the first time Jesse had been naked in front of more than one person at a time and, when he first arrived, he considered darting behind a rock to take his clothes off. But if you were going to come out from the rock naked, what was the point of hiding while you disrobed? The main pool, which was cooler than the smaller one a little higher up, was filled with about half women and half men. None of them seemed the slightest bit anxious about the fact that their private parts were on display for the world to judge. Too skinny? Too fat? Too many weird tattoos? No tattoos? Jesse was sure he wasn't supposed to be having these sort of thoughts, but what else could he think about?

Maya was settled into the smaller, hot pool, and deep into an intricate-sounding conversation about Monsanto, detailing some debate she had helped organize between a representative from the European Food Safety Authority and the FDA over genetically modified foods. She didn't even seem to notice that the man she was having this heavy discussion with was sitting on the edge of the pool with a pierced penis right about level with her head. Jesse greeted her, but didn't bother to feel the water; he knew he couldn't hang in the hot pool.

He doddled with his clothes for a while then finally just pulled them off, folding them neatly so his wallet didn't make a noticeable bulge, and went gingerly over to the larger pool, his bare feet protesting the rocky path. He wanted to just dangle his feet in the cooler pool, which was still a million degrees too hot, but couldn't fathom trying to talk to anyone there with his not pierced and very small (but potentially uncomfortably and uncontrollably growing) penis exposed, so he jumped in and sunk down until the water hit his neck. The woman next to him gave him a slightly annoyed smile; maybe he'd splashed her. Maybe she was hoping for someone sexier.

After about ten minutes of awkward silence while Jesse watched as one of the women floated another around the middle of the pool on her back—her large, luscious breasts sailing above the waterline like the blatant advertisements they were—Jesse had no choice but to sit up on the edge. He felt exactly how a lobster must feel. He looked up at the smaller pool, wondering if Maya was ready to leave. Earlier he'd overheard that guy tell her that there must be something miraculous going on, because he'd had a dream about her last night, "It was like my entire body recognizes everything about you!" Jesse would have gone up there to perform some sort of he-man "she is mine" act, but Maya obviously didn't need his help and, frankly, she wasn't his. Plus, he couldn't imagine putting one toe in the hot pool if this scalding insanity was the cool pool. Then the woman who had been floated around like a prize pig popped up in front of him and, placing her hands gently over her chest, asked coyly, "Were you staring at my heart?"

Before Jesse could get out an, "um, yeah," she turned around and announced to the pool that she felt moved to teach a yoga class—would anyone care to join? Jesse and every other man in that pool immediately agreed. For those tits he would forget how uncomfortable he was and do a downward dog— penis, ball sack, and asshole exposed and available for all the world.

After a few sun salutations, she told them all to lie on the warm rocks and close their eyes for a mental relaxation exercise. They visualized the ocean waves splashing up on their toes and then receding, the next wave crashing higher up to their knees and receding, and once the last wave washed over their heads, they entered into an underwater world where they were surrounded with warmth and love and they easily sank deeper...and deeper...and deeper.

Jesse wanted to comment that he was so relaxed he could officially check meditate off his list for the day, but it didn't feel like a joke moment, so he decided to hold it until he had a chance to ask for her number later. She told them to try her relaxation technique at home when trying to fall asleep. Focusing on the waves would distract you away from the otherwise endless whirl of brain chatter. The trick, she said, was to make sure your tongue was relaxed at the end. If your waves were all crashed out but your tongue was pressed hard against the top of your mouth, you'd never fall asleep.

***

Jesse was awake. He knew he was awake. But he was spacing out, thinking about his tongue, and the girl that taught that yoga class. He had started imagining what their tongues could do when they weren't relaxing. She had a little too much weight on her hips to be convincing as a yoga master, and a little too much new-agey speak to be convincing as anything else, but she was his kind of fuck-able. He was wondering if she would have given him her phone number if he'd had the nerve to ask. Not that *that* matters. Not that any of this matters, Jesse reminded himself.

After the crash he kept thinking about the yoga girl, though, as if the horrific grinding of metal on metal, the loud noise, the blood and the pure, raw fear had branded her image into his mind because that was the last random thing he'd thought before it happened. It was as if his brain kept wanting to escape reality, turn back time, and return to that last moment. So there it stayed, a mental picture of her tanned, round ass, taunting him as proof of how selfish he truly was. How basically untrustworthy he was, so desperate to move on to the next fuck, so preoccupied with the last fuck, or the fuck that got away, that he couldn't be relied upon to even pay attention to the fucking road in front of him.

Since he didn't have the pleasure of passing out after the accident (damn airbags!) the police took a statement from him right there on the scene. Right as they were racing Maya off to a hospital, her legs so bloody and contorted and broken it took at least five people to extract her from the car and move her to a gurney, the police asked Jesse what happened. He looked at the young officer, who had sat down next to him on the guardrail, who had an earnest look on his face with maybe a tinge of fear. For a full minute Jesse just stared ahead at scattered broken glass on the pavement, and fought to get control of his mind, to eradicate the image of that stupid yoga chick and try to focus on the question. What happened? What happened was that I care more about my dick than other human beings, he though nastily to himself. But Jesse had dealt with cops before; he knew he had to choose his words carefully, to look past his haze of guilt, to spin the facts to his advantage. He was the only witness, after all. He had come around the corner and there was an abandoned car in his lane. It was dark. He was under the speed limit. He didn't have enough time to stop, Jesse told the cops. But was it true? Did he have enough time to stop?

Later, sitting in the hospital waiting room, Jesse thought of those words, *enough time*, as either a cop-out or a guilt trip, depending on how much he hated himself in that particular moment. He had felt like there wasn't enough time in his life to waste an extra day on that road trip with Maya. But he was healthy, he was fine, and now it was Maya who might not have enough time. If he hadn't been in such a hurry to get to California, he wouldn't have been in that situation. He wouldn't have needed enough time to stop. He wasn't paying attention. He was thinking about a fat yoga bottom, ignoring the fact that he wasn't in prime driving condition, and racing toward some imaginary sex buffet happening that very moment in San Francisco. If he had been driving slower, or if he had kept his mind in the present tense, he would have seen that car. He would have been able to swerve around it. There were two lanes; he didn't need "enough time" to stop. Sitting in the waiting room of the hospital, the bright lights casting gloomy shadows on its sad, tired inhabitants, waiting hours for news from Maya's surgeons. For the first time in his adult life, Jesse felt glad that San Francisco was still miles away. He didn't deserve to go there, he hated who he would have become there. Maya's trove of surgeons probably would have no choice but to cut what remained of her legs off, and Jesse was sitting on a plastic chair, with nothing but time.

"Jesse?" the nurse called out, "Is there a Jesse here?" Jesse jumped to his feet, spilling a little of the coffee from his Styrofoam cup. "I'm Jesse," he responded. "Is Maya okay?" Guilt stabbed him in the stomach. He knew she wasn't okay. How could she be okay? But he couldn't bring himself to ask if she was alive. Less than twenty-four hours ago there was blood gushing out of her everywhere, the right pant leg of Jesse's jeans were still stiff and black with her dried blood. She could be dead.

"Well, she has been through a lot, but she is stabilized now, and her doctor wants to give her body a rest before the next surgery," the nurse replied, her tropical print shirt providing a garish counterpoint to the horror of the situation. Then she added, just in case it wasn't obvious, "She is going to need several surgeries. You'll have to speak with the doctor to learn more. She is awake now, though, and she said she wants to speak with you."

Jesse followed the nurse through the hall, each door shut tight or yawning open with its own bloody story to tell. Jesse shivered. He hated hospitals. He thought of Maya wrapped up on that gurney, her blood already soaking through the blanket they put over the tattered remains of her legs. She had fainted by then, but her screams still hung in the air like angry ghosts.

When he walked into the room, the sheets covering Maya were white. He couldn't see any blood or anything of her body below her chest. The entire mess was neatly tucked away with hospital corners.

"Oh my God, Maya, I am so, so sorry," he said as he went over to the bed. She had a large Band-Aid over her left eye; was it damaged in the crash, too? He didn't remember. Did she lose her eye?!

"What happened, Jesse? I can't remember. I was asleep..."

"There was an abandoned car left on the highway. I don't know anything more about it. I don't know why it was there. I didn't see it until it was too late, but Maya, this is my fault. I shouldn't have been driving that late. I can't tell you how sorry I am. Did they tell you anything about your legs? Will you be okay? What is going on with your eye?" Jesse's words heaved out of him like vomit, leaving bile-flavored guilt on his tongue, but he forced himself to shut up after he really looked at her. Maya was struggling to stay awake.

"The doctors say that I need another surgery," she said, her voice weak with exhaustion and pain medication, "I feel confused, Jesse. One of them said something about an infection. Or maybe it was a risk of infection. And my legs, I think they said I don't have enough blood in my legs... I'm so tired, but I had to see you. I need you to do something for me."

"Anything."

CHAPTER SIXTEEN

THE KNOCK AT the door was unexpected. Who would be stopping by at nine at night? Except for a few wild nights in her teens, Jean had rarely dealt with any member of the public after 8:00 p.m. She was already in her pajamas watching TV and eating the cookies she kept hidden on the top shelf of the bathroom closet. Marvin was asleep; he had to get up for a five a.m. Pranayama training session—a one-time opportunity to learn from some famous guru passing through town. Pranayama is basically a bunch of people in a room breathing in loud, snorty ways. Marvin said that offering Pranayama classes at the Divine Center was critical to keeping up with the trends, and a step ahead of the competition over at Lotus Studios. Marvin had been a constant help since the baby was born, but Jean was annoyed that he would have to leave her, even for a few hours, to struggle through Sienna's morning routine, which coincides exactly with the hour that Arvin likes to wake up and cry. But she hadn't complained to him because, frankly, they needed Marvin's income. If Santa Cruz housewives want to pay someone to learn how to breathe, Jean wanted it to be her husband that took the money.

Standing on the other side of the door was a scruffy young man, early twenties, clearly a homeless gutter punk. Jean had seen his type many times before. Santa Cruz had loads of these kids, sitting down on Pacific Avenue, thinking of creative ways to beg for cash. Some of them played easy-to-transport instruments like tambourines or recorders, but most just held up signs saying things like "spare a dollar, spare a life," "contribute to my adventure," or Jean's favorite: "buy me a beer." Jean used to give a dollar here and there to help them prolong the innocence of youth. She and Marvin probably would have done some big adventuring of their own if they hadn't had Maverick. But about a year ago, Jean was driving into the Home Depot parking lot, passing by the five or six Mexican men who regularly hung out there waiting for an honest day's work, when she noticed a young white man standing on the other corner holding a sign that said "Spare Change My day." Jean wanted to take a picture and post it to show what was wrong with American youth. Here were these immigrants working their butts off, day in and day out, doing menial tasks for small amounts of cash, while that entitled brat expected the world to just hand him money. Since then she had stopped giving out cash to kids. She had other charities, like Legal Aid, that actually served society instead of expecting society to serve them. Sometimes the street kids were overly pushy, acting like she was the rude one if she refused give them her hard-earned money. But she had never seen one begging door to door.

"Yes?" Jean said after opening the door a crack and peering through, her body tensing with preparation for the "no" she was about to say.

"Are you Jean Simmons?" Jesse asked.

"Yes..."

"I'm Jesse Hawthorn. It's nice to meet you. Um, I need to talk to you."

"Okay," Jean said, not opening the door wider. "What about?"

"May I come in? This is kinda private," Jesse said, looking around at the quiet, empty street.

"Well, I don't know you, so why don't you tell me the nature of this issue you are having and I'll decide." Jean used her courtroom voice. She was not going to let this scruff-ball into her house and expose her babies to danger. She was already thinking about how fast she could bolt over to where she'd left her phone on the end table if she needed to dial 9-1-1.

"It's about Maya. She's hurt. She wanted me to give you something," he said looking stressed, or was it guilty? Jean quickly opened the door and pointed to the couch, sitting herself in the uncomfortable blue striped chair she usually offered guests when she didn't want them to stay long. She needed to sit up straight for this. Just the mention of Maya's name sent a cold chill of fear down her spine, like the very word had the capacity to further the erosion between Sienna and Jean. Sienna had been a complete mess that day. When Jean picked her up from school she said she wanted to go to the cafe and get an ice cream. Sienna was a sugar fanatic, and the devil spice drives her batty so Jean tries to limit consumption. Sienna asking for ice cream after school and Jean turning her down was part of their regular routine, but today Sienna had thrown a huge fit and said Jean was the "most terrible, baddest mommy in the whole wide world!" and she hoped that "a huge, gigantic dinosaur" would come and eat her. Sienna was going through a major adjective phase. She was also going through a pushing boundaries phase. One of the ones Jean was trying to hold strong on was the rule against being disrespectful, but it was exhausting.

Jean told Sienna that she was allowed to say she was mad at Mommy but she was not allowed to say mean things. Sienna retorted that she could say any mean thing she wanted because she was a "mean little girl," which, of course launched Jean into a self-inflicted guilt trip: Did Sienna have this new self-image because she hadn't been getting enough attention? Jean counted her sins: (1) Leaving Sienna at preschool until 4:00 or 5:00 p.m. while Jean enjoyed quiet time in her office and the new baby slept. (2) Putting Sienna in front of the TV instead of playing with her so Jean could sit and nurse the baby. Jean wanted to make up for the fact that Sienna didn't come out of her own womb. She had stayed home for a year and even attempted to breastfeed Sienna, but (3) she couldn't shake the deep-down feeling that Sienna was marginalized by the circumstances of her birth. Sienna needed more, and now that the baby was here, Jean had even less to give. So Jean gave in and bought the ice cream. Marvin would never know, but his voice rang loudly in Jean's head that the girl had Jean wrapped around her finger, and Jean better grow a spine or Sienna would run right over her when she turned thirteen. All Marvin saw was a normal three-year-old testing boundaries and a mother who didn't know how to hold strong. How lovely it must be to have such a simplistic, unemotional view when what Jean saw, or more accurately, what Jean felt, were widening cracks in the delicate cement between her and her precious little girl, cracks she was desperately inadequate to fill.

There had been a car crash and Maya was injured, Jesse was saying. Maya had to have a surgery. Something about her legs, her eye. She might not survive. Jesse's words were tumbling out, and Jean had to force herself to focus.

"She wants Sienna to have her locket," Jesse said, producing a small gold heart with the Star of David carved into the top.

"What? Hold on." Jean suddenly became hyper

alert. "Is she going to live?"

"The doctor said that sometimes people get infections. It could be lethal," Jesse said, with all the seriousness of a young man who had never seen a medical crisis before. Then he cringed, as if Jean was about to hit him. What was with this guy and his obvious guilt? Did he hurt Maya?

"Well, there is always the risk of infection in surgeries. I'm sure she'll be fine, if that's the only worry. Do you know anything more about the prognosis?" Jean asked.

"If she makes it though the surgery, I guess it will be a slow recovery. She lost a lot of blood. They are putting a lot of metal in her legs and they have to amputate at least one foot. Her parents are flying up from Peru," he said. Jean remembered the parents, Kai better than Sandy. Kai was one of those blond, dreadlocked guys—a "honky rasta" Marvin had joked. When Maya was in labor, Kai had hung out with them in the waiting room, stinking of weed and arguing with Marvin that Bikram yoga was commercialized, American crap that was spreading like a disease to undermine true, spiritual forms of yoga. Sandy and Kai had gone backpacking in India when Maya was young, and he thought he was the authority on all things Hindu. That poor girl had been hauled to street corners around the globe. No wonder Maverick was attracted to her. He had considered majoring in Cultural Studies before he discovered Animal Sciences. Maya lived cultural studies.

"Well... let me know, okay? I'll give you my number," Jean said, rushing Jesse to the door, well aware of the fact that he probably had no place to stay. She just wanted him out. She picked up a piece of junk mail from where it had landed on the floor under the mail slot earlier and wrote her number down.

"Um, here, take the locket. Maya wanted, I mean she wants Sienna to have it." He pushed the small thing into Jean's hand before going out the door. Jean could see that he wanted to talk more, that he probably needed someone to talk to, but she couldn't deal with trying to be kind. The locket burned in her hand and she needed to be alone, to sit down and try to figure out what to do with it.

CHAPTER SEVENTEEN

"SO, HOW DID you get into this mess" Kai Barsky asked, taking a drag on the joint and then passing it casually to Jesse, like he assumed Jesse was an old-time marijuana smoker, Jesse noted with a touch of undeserved pride. He could count the times he had smoked weed on his fingers, and maybe a few toes, so he could hardly claim the title, or the tolerance. But he was careful to follow Kai's method, and kept the smoke inside his lungs for a few extra seconds to fully absorb the drug. The smoke made his head swirl and irritated his throat, and he immediately started coughing.

Jesse looked over at Kai to see if his image was blown. Back in DC, the kids would laugh and say that coughing meant that this was "good shit," but Kai didn't say anything about it. He just looked at

Jesse expectantly, waiting for an answer to his question. Jesse figured that Kai wanted to know if Jesse and Maya were serious, if they were a couple, or whatever, but he didn't have an answer for Kai. At least not an answer that Jesse thought Kai might like. Dads are so protective of their daughters, probably even a hippy dad doesn't want to think that his daughter was having casual sex. And, in the end, that's what it was, Jesse could see that now. Casual sex with maybe a flicker of friendship brewing. Jesse was about to open his mouth to emphasize the friendship aspect, when it occurred to him that maybe he was misreading Kai. Maybe the man just really wanted to know how Jesse got into this mess.

"It sounds cheesy, but I guess I was trying to find myself," Jesse said finally, and then braced for the laugh, because how fucking overplayed was that line? Or maybe he was afraid Kai would drop the mellow hippy charade, turn towards him and just punch him. Hard, in the face. The thought of a raging, maniacal Kai caused Jesse to giggle a little. Then guilt spun in like the smoke swirling around his head. He imagined staring at his own reflection in a mirror like a crazed narcissist while Maya's leg was being cut off in the background, unnoticed, her screams muted. At this point getting beat up by Kai would feel good, a relief, Jesse realized. Maybe that was why he was giggling like a fucking idiot, like a sixteen-year-old smoking his uncle's marijuana stash in the attic, giggling with fear over being caught.

"Finding yourself is a good goal, Jesse, and if you don't mind, I have a suggestion for you on that task."

"Really? I'm up for suggestions. I've hit a dead end on my own here."

Kai took another hit and leaned back on the park bench they'd scouted out in People's Park, a particular bench that took them almost an hour to walk to but was, for some fond memories reason, important to Kai. "The first step in finding yourself is to get rid of the things you are not. Take me, for example. When I was young, I thought that I needed to become management in a factory, like my father, only I wasn't management material. I thought I wanted a house in the suburbs with a white picket fence, only I didn't like the suburbs. I thought I wanted a new car, but what I really loved was to ride my bicycle. I had to throw out these goals before I could figure out what my real goals were. Once I did that, the world opened up. At first, all I knew was that I loved my bicycle. So I started riding it. I rode and rode and rode until I was traveling around the country by bicycle.

"And then I met Sandy. I was riding my bicycle down the Pacific Highway and stopped off in a little town known for great weed. We'd spend long afternoons warming our naked selves on the banks of the beautiful rivers around there. Smoking weed, swapping stories. Sandy was the second thing that I knew I wanted. But after I had her, we didn't know where to go from there. One bicycle, two people. She was also in the process of peeling off the shit to find the diamond on the inside. She had a husband at the time who was going to save the trees and the birds and the rest of the universe with his guitar, but who couldn't save himself from alcoholism. Like most of the women in that town, Sandy had fallen in love with the idea of this jerk, but only Sandy had to deal with the reality behind closed doors. He beat her. I wanted to save her, but what was I going to do? Put her on my handlebars and ride away? So I thought about it for a few days, then sold the bike and bought us bus fare to Oakland."

"And you lived there? What did you do?" Jesse was suddenly overwhelmed with gratitude. Kai was being nice to him, telling him stories, letting Jesse know him. In fact, Jesse loved old stories, especially free-love hippy stories. Why oh why wasn't I born in that generation? he thought. A love-in would have been right up Jesse's alley. At least before the crash.

"Well, we didn't weave daises in our hair and sell poems from the street corner, if that's what you think. I got a job, like any man trying to support his woman. I got a job framing houses in the hot sun and I was happy to have it. Sandy started working in a new age shop, selling incense and tarot cards. We got a cruddy little apartment in Emeryville, and we made do until we could figure out the next thing."

"What was the next thing?"

"Maya," he said with an end of the story tone that Jesse wanted immediately to subvert with another question, but he held himself back. People like to talk about themselves, but they don't like it when you pry. There was a fine line there that Jesse had crossed before. Maybe Kai was only being cool with him because he'd found the weed dealer. Kai had called up a few of his old friends but hadn't been able to score. Jesse needed to do whatever he could to help, and could see that Kai's need was immediate, so he went over to the university and asked the most likely person he saw: another white guy with blond dreadlocks (they're all over around here, but when Jesse made a joke about it, Maya curtly informed him that very few of these "hippies" were actually from California). Jesse had felt a little weird about asking a total stranger for weed; it was still illegal in DC. But Kai's daughter would never walk again on two feet because of Jesse. Giving Kai a few moments of drug-induced peace was the least he could do.

Before Jesse handed him a joint, Kai had barely noticed Jesse in the panic of his and Sandy's arrival, talking to the doctors, crying with Maya. Jesse had almost left. Who was he to be a part of these intimate family moments? Except, he had caused the crash. Or at least not avoided it. And nobody invited him to leave, which he guessed he needed. Instead, they invited him to stay with them at their friend's empty house in the Berkeley hills, probably assuming that there was more between Maya and him than one increasingly fucked-up road trip, and Jesse, not knowing what else to do, had guiltily accepted.

The past few days of sitting in the hospital

waiting room, drinking black cafeteria coffee, had at least given him some time for reflection on the string of mistakes he'd made that caused him to end up there. The mistakes compounded themselves exponentially, and now seemed to have acquired such mass that they had their own gravitational pull. He had no idea how to get free.

Hooking up with the hottest woman he could find at a gay club because he was too chicken shit to hook up with a man; that was the first mistake. It seemed so stupid now. Convincing himself that he was in love with a stranger because she had the childhood he wanted; his second mistake. Getting stuck on a cross-country adventure with a know-it-all pre-law compounded the first two. Then, because she had fallen off the pedestal he'd put her on in the first place and he was too hurried for the next thing to take much heed of her safety, he almost killed her. Almost *killed* her in a mad dash to get back to another gay club and try again.

Now she would never dance in a club again, not on two feet anyway. Maybe "gravitational pull" wasn't the right term. He had dove headlong into a shithole, and the stink would probably be with him forever because of nothing more and nothing less than selfishness.

Guilt kept Jesse glued to the Barsky family, but after a few days, curiosity seeped in as well. Who were Kai and Sandy? Wild haired and relaxed, they reminded Jesse of no one he'd ever met. He'd met plenty of neo-hippies—people who followed bands or festivals, their "unique" look so ubiquitous it was obvious to everyone but them that they followed a strict dress code. But Kai and Sandy were different. They were the real deal. The way they talked, moved, probably their very pulse, seemed slower than everyone around them. They were centered. Even facing this crisis, the devastating fact that their only daughter would never walk on two feet again, they talked of gratitude and peace.

Jesse had overheard Sandy say to Maya that perhaps the injury was an invitation to her to reevaluate her life. To slow down and take note of the important things. Perhaps it was a blessing from the Great Spirit (she actually said that): a gift to be cherished rather than feared. Jesse checked to see if Maya was rolling her eyes, but she wasn't. The words of her mother soothed her, as they have done for injured children throughout time.

Sandy wasn't just trying to soothe, though. She and Kai had come with an agenda, and made themselves clear the moment they arrived. They wanted Maya to recuperate with them in Peru. As free-spirited as they were, they were still parents, and it was clear that they had never been fully stoked on Maya living so far away in DC. So far away from them.

Jesse had slunk into the corner of the hospital room during an argument between Maya and Sandy the day after Sandy and Kai arrived. Maya was saying that there were good physical therapists in DC and Sandy was countering, "But do they live with you? Who will walk you to the bathroom, Maya? What if you need help to pee? What if you fall in the night?" After a week it seemed that Maya was wearing down. She admitted that swimming in the ocean would be good for building up her strength; you don't need two feet for swimming.

"I guess this is it for my big dreams of seeing Sienna," Maya said to Jesse with a sarcastic tone that failed to cover her pain. She had gotten so close. Just a two-hour drive, but it was a million miles away now. They'd missed the meet date, of course, and Jean didn't exactly invite them over when Jesse went to deliver the necklace. Earlier in the summer Jean had told Maya that she needed to get there before the baby was due, and Jesse got the distinct impression that she still felt that way. The baby had arrived and the door had closed, if it ever was open in the first place. When Jesse returned from Santa Cruz, he hesitated to tell Maya about the cold welcome he'd received from Jean.

He could see that the woman obviously wanted nothing to do with Maya, so he embellished just a tiny bit, saying that Jean had promised to give the locket to Sienna and that she hoped Maya would still visit when she was well. But Maya must have seen through the lie; she hasn't called Jean. Thinking about this made Jesse angry. It wasn't Maya's fault she was riding with a selfish jerk who crashed the car. Jean shouldn't punish her because of him. And what about the little girl? Didn't Jean think it might be a good thing for Sienna to meet her biological mother? A mother who was so desperate to meet her, Jesse now realized, that she gave up a career-building internship and risked her life traveling across the country with some punk she barely knew, but who could pay for the trip, just to see the child she knew she could never have back.

And now it wasn't going to happen. Maya was headed to Peru as soon as the doctors said she could travel. Her parents had no interest in taking a side trip to where they were unwanted, to visit another one of their daughter's mistakes. "You need to focus on the positive, on moving forward," Sandy softly advised her daughter. "That shit is just going to stress her out," Kai said to Jesse when he suggested that they all drive down to Santa Cruz.

Maybe Kai was right, Jesse thought. Maybe the stress of an awkward meeting with Sienna would hurt Maya even more, but he had to risk it. He'd promised to take Maya to see her daughter, and right now keeping that promise was the only path he had to making amends for her missing foot and, maybe, putting his mistakes to bed.

If only Jean would bring Sienna to see Maya, Jesse could go home, he thought. Not to the party block in Adam's Morgan, but to Reston, Virginia, the suburb he grew up in. His schemes of living some mightier than thou alternative life felt empty now. Rather than a great philosopher or writer, he was just a horny, selfish kid that let fantasy obscure reality. No better than the neo-hippy festival goers, or even the Georgetown law students he used to make fun of.

He was worse, actually, he thought, because while they reached deep within their souls to grasp at their favorite jam band or that law degree, Jesse sat on the sidelines, being so cool, laughing at everyone else while his own heart's desires languished, unanalyzed, in some dusty corner. Then, when he finally sought them out, he tripped over his own ego, missed them completely, and ruined someone else's life.

Jesse had always thought that he wanted a story like Kai's for himself. Kai's great breakout from the doldrums of the suburbs was exactly how Jesse saw his own life path. Kai had followed what was true in his heart, what really called to him. Scorning middle management for an endless bike ride was a perfect ending to a life story, from Jesse's perspective. But, that wasn't the end, or even the most important part of Kai's story, Jesse realized now. When Kai found an opportunity to help someone, he had responded unselfishly. Or maybe selling his bike to care for an abused woman and then working long hours in construction to support a family was what Kai's heart had wanted all along. Jesse's head spun with confusion, and the confusion made him feel exhausted.

Maybe what Kai had wanted was an authentic life. Jesse wanted an authentic life. But what does that really mean? Other than to be undisputedly, magnificently cool, and therefore loved, he didn't have a clue. Suddenly the past two years of partying in Adam's Morgan seemed hollow, too. What was he doing all that time? What was the point? He wasn't even really sure he wanted to be a writer anymore. Other than the letters to Slaven, he hardly ever felt like picking up his pen. Maybe he had just thought that a writer was a cool thing to be, or maybe he just wanted to connect with Slaven. Or maybe telling himself that he was going to be a writer helped him ignore the fact that he was nothing at all.

Not knowing what he wanted out of life was the reason why his attempt to "break out" was convoluted and strained, Jesse decided. It was jinxed from the get-go because he had only been pretending that he was a passionate, interesting person with dreams to follow. Of course, it seemed obvious to him now, his clumsy grab for superiority was bound to result in someone getting hurt. A wave of nausea and exhaustion swept over Jesse. Maybe it was the after effects of the marijuana, but Jesse was overcome with the desire to go home, maybe to face reality, or maybe to climb into his childhood bed and close the door. But, until then, he wanted only to be helpful.

"Hey," Jesse called to Kai, who was now stretched out with his eyes closed in a sunny spot on the grass. The last of the joint, still loosely clasped between his thumb and pointer finger, had gone cold. "I have a few things to do. Can I meet you back at the hospital?"

As soon as he was out of earshot, Jesse called Jean on the GoPhone he'd bought a few days earlier. Between grocery runs for the Barskys and hospital updates, being unavailable was not a luxury he could afford anymore. By some miracle, Jean answered on the second ring. He told her that Maya wouldn't be able to go there, that she and Sienna were invited to visit the hospital. He ignored Jean's excuses (the baby, the baby, the baby) and insisted that it would be good for Maya's recovery to see Sienna. She had time, he told her. Maya could be in the hospital for at least another week. He wouldn't get off the phone before she agreed to think about it.

CHAPTER EIGHTEEN

SIENNA AND BABY Arvin were sleeping like angels in the backseat. There is nothing more beautiful than a sleeping child. Just glancing in her rearview mirror was enough to nearly burst Jean's heart open with love, which was an entirely different feeling than the one she'd had ten minutes ago when both children were screaming bloody murder and she couldn't figure out, for the life of her, why she chose to have two children so close together in age. Not that there was any advance planning associated with any of her children. Sometimes Jean joked with Marvin that her secret code name was Queen Oops Baby Mamma. But, looking at them now, so sweet, so perfect, Jean knew she couldn't have planned it better.

"They're both asleep!" Jean whispered to Wynn,

who was sitting child-free in the passenger seat of Jean's Subaru. Jean was so glad that Wynn agreed to come on this trip. For the past few weeks Jean had been obsessing over Maya during their daily stroller "walk and talks," which they took along West Cliff drive at dawn. The idea was that if they were home before seven a.m., when their older children were likely to wake up, they could get an hour of exercise, girlfriend therapy, and "me" time before their husbands had to deal with too much morning fuss all by their lonesomes. "Thank you so much for coming. I know spending a day with my kids is not exactly the ideal choice for your big first day away from your kids."

"No problem. This is a big deal. I want to support you. You know, I was just thinking about all that crying. If they aren't your kids, it really doesn't affect you the same way. It's weird. When Oliver and Julien cry it's like a dagger stabbing at me. My anxiety goes through the roof and I feel panicked to make them happy again. But just now when Sienna and Arvin were crying, it really didn't bother me so much... not that I don't adore your kids!" Wynn laughed.

"Oh, I know! It's like moms are hardwired for their own child's cry. I guess it makes sense. If we didn't feel such a rush of adrenalin when our baby cries, we might run away from it rather than toward it!"

"So what did you end up telling Sienna about Maya?" Wynn asked. They'd already had a long discussion about this. Jean had debated about what to say for days. She wanted to have some sort of age-appropriate honesty with Sienna, but she didn't even really know what Maya was like, or what she wanted. On the telephone Jesse said that Maya was moving to Peru in a few days, and so this might be the last chance Sienna would have to see her, maybe for years. But Jesse was the same kid who said Maya was dying before in the hospital, so he was obviously prone to exaggeration. Peru wasn't that far away. And didn't she go to college in DC? She couldn't be finished with that yet. And Maya didn't even call. Jean thought that it was very odd that Maya kept sending her boyfriend to communicate. Jesse made it sound like she was pretty hurt, but not in a coma or anything. How badly does she want to see Sienna if she didn't even call herself?

"I haven't told her anything, really. I don't want Sienna to get too excited about this new, um, other mother, and then feel disappointed if she never sees her again. I just want to feel it out a little bit first. She's only three. I'm hoping I can introduce Maya by name and leave it at that. Would you look at the directions again? Jesse said that navigation might not work very well out here in the hills."

"I think it's fine. It's telling us to turn on Sherman, and that's what you wrote down," Wynn said, looking at the envelope Jean had jotted the directions on. "Where are we going, anyway? Is there a hospital out here?" Wynn asked, looking around at trees and grass.

"I guess her parents have a friend or something with a place and they've been staying there the past few weeks. Maya left the hospital a day or so ago, but their flight to Peru isn't for a few days. Jesse said that she is recovering pretty slowly, and they're running tests."

"Is she in a wheel chair?" Wynn asked.

"Maybe, I'm not sure. She lost her foot in the crash, but I guess they'll give her a prosthetic."

"How awful! Poor thing. I can't imagine being so young and losing a limb. I bet she's totally depressed," Wynn said.

"Yeah, I guess I've been so consumed with how all of this affects me that it hadn't occurred to me to feel sorry for her."

"You're really doing a good deed bringing Sienna to her."

"I don't know, Wynn. She might not even care about seeing Sienna. She didn't call. I don't even know if she was ever really planning on visiting. Maybe visiting us in California was just an afterthought, like if she made it that far on her road trip."

"Jean, from the way you described that first telephone call it sounded like seeing Sienna was a pretty high priority for her. Maya is a kind of mother. Even flakey teenagers are hardwired to love the babies they birth."

"I guess you're right. Sorry. Maybe I want her to be evil, or unloving, or somehow bad. Someone Sienna could never love. But that's only part of me.

The other part of me wants Maya to be loving, and perfect, and fairy godmother-like because I know Sienna will want to love her either way. And she is going to recognize that Maya is a part of her. I don't want Sienna to see Maya's flaws and think they are her own... Damn, I'm a mess! I can't wait until this day is over," Jean said as a minivan passed them on the right, honking its objection to her left lane cruising. Jean pulled into the right lane and was immediately passed by the five cars that had been (politely) waiting for her to pull her shit together.

"Twelve hours and counting. You're going to get through it, I promise!" Wynn reached over and squeezed Jean's hand. I am so lucky to have her in my life, Jean thought. Sometimes it was the new friends, who appeared out of thin air just when you most needed them, that were made of gold.

"Are you sure this is it?" Jean asked Wynn as they pulled up to a ten-foot-tall gate with a large gilded whale swimming in the ironwork overhead.

"Um, yes. Wow," Wynn replied, as the gate sensed their presence and slowly swung open. Beyond it was a white gravel road winding softly through a field landscaped with native plants and blue-gray boulders. Or at least Jean assumed they were native plants, because they fit so perfectly, and she assumed the boulders were landscaped as well because, well, they fit so perfectly.

Orange and golden California poppies littered the field like cupcake sprinkles along with some pretty blue flower Jean couldn't name, various types of sages, and tall grasses that waved elegantly in the breeze their car made as they drove past. It was a perfect, sunny, blue-sky day, and both of them caught their breath as they rounded a grove of oak trees and a full sweeping view of the San Francisco Bay came into view.

The Golden Gate Bridge, in all its architectural glory, was directly in front of them at the far end of the glistening bay. The Golden Gate Bridge had always been Jean's favorite. To her, the gift from the bridge's creators wasn't just the beauty of the bridge itself, but a reminder of the daily choice we all make between creating function, and creating functional art. Be it mothering, writing briefs, being a friend, building a house, or any other activity under the sun, we have the choice at every moment to try for a functional result, or a glorious life. The Golden Gate Bridge was the glorious life and, looking at it now, Jean had the same reaction she always had: a burst of joy expanding in her chest. Maybe today wouldn't be so bad after all.

"Sienna, Sienna sweetie, wake up. We're here! You have to see this view!" Jean whispered into her daughter's ear as she unbuckled her seatbelt. Sienna sleepily let Jean move the straps off her shoulders and put her arms up for Jean to carry her. Jean swung Sienna onto her hip and pointed to the vast amount of air creating magic between them and the hundreds of thousands of people inhabiting the areas below.

"What is that?" she asked, pointing to the

peninsula.

"Those are skyscrapers in San Francisco," Jean said.

"I know about San Frisco!" she said. "I have a bus and a trolley and a train there!"

"Good remembering!" They'd been to the Golden Gate Park, a restaurant right next to Ocean Beach, and a few museums, but of course what Sienna remembered first was the thrill of riding the bus.

"I want to go to San Frisco. Can we go now? Beautiful pleeeease? Now!" she asked. The whine creeping into her voice was like fingernails scraping a chalkboard on Jean's already frayed nerves, but Jean was determined to keep her temper. I will be a perfect, absolutely love-filled mother today, Jean reminded herself.

"No, sweetie, we're visiting friends today. Look at this wonderful house we get to explore!" Jean shifted her attention away from the view towards the unique mansion next to them. It had several rounded roofs covered in aged redwood shingles so that the whole building looked like a pile of silver-toned bubbles. Parts of it were backed into the hillside behind it. Jean was curious about what they did to protect the shingled part of the roof from the grass part. Scattered about the domes were huge rounded windows. There was so much glass that, if there were neighbors, they could see right into every room. But the house was surrounded only by the oak grove and air. It must be worth a fortune.

"How do you like the place?" greeted Kai when

they went to the door. "I like to call it 'Hippy Fruition'."

"You've got that right! Wow. Who owns this place?" Jean asked, allowing the grandiose surroundings to overwhelm normative greetings.

"It's a record producer friend of mine who got his start finding talent in the Grateful Dead parking lots. He used to live here but his old lady wants to live in the city, so he loans it out for retreats. Cool dude. He's letting us stay here *gratis* until Maya is ready to travel."

"Oh. How is she doing?"

"She's been out of the hospital for a couple days now. We thought we could get her out of here already, but she has got a whole arsenal of doctors and therapists that insist on seeing her constantly. I think they see that good university health insurance and start drooling. I swear if they'd just let her relax she'd heal much faster. That's why we're taking her back with us to Peru. She needs to be in a peaceful place."

"Are there good doctors where you live in Peru?" Jean asked, trying to keep her voice neutral. Jean would be the first one to admit that she doesn't know much about Peru, but Kai's opinion that relaxing on the beach was better than physical therapy for someone who just lost a foot sounded a little naive. Not that she wasn't thrilled that Maya was leaving.

"Sure, but even better there is this chiropractor who practiced in LA for twenty years before he moved down. Everyone swears by him. And, let me tell you, he won't try to dope Maya up on pain killers like the doctors here... but, of course, if Maya needs them, they're easy to get." Kai winked at Jean and smiled, indicating that he could get just about anything anyone needed from certain pharmacies in Peru. A wave of repulsion hit Jean in the stomach. She had lived in Northern California her whole life so tall, tan, blond men with dreadlocks swaying down their back were nothing new to her, but Kai was just *so* cliché. Jean vaguely remembered that he was originally from the Midwest somewhere, and he definitely looked like he'd descended from some Nordic god, a corn-fed Midwesterner. Jean could understand the big thrill of moving out to California in your twenties, growing your hair out and being wild for a time, but it was like Kai never caught the memo that eventually you need to grow up. Somehow Maya turned out fairly sensible though, at least she seemed that way during the pregnancy, when Jean was spending so much time with her. Jean remembered Maya researching the correct pregnancy diet and the best supplements. Maverick had mentioned that she was good in school, too.

Jean swallowed her judgments and introduced Kai to Sienna and Wynn, who was holding sleeping Arvin in his heavy infant car seat. Kai was sweet to Sienna, crouching down to her level to ask her about the ride. Sienna told him about "her" trains and busses in "San Frisco" and he acted genuinely impressed. "I've always wanted a train! You know, when I was your age I loved trains so much that I would beg my mom to run with me over to the tracks every time I'd hear one coming. And where I live now I get to ride super fancy busses with TVs inside." His comment sent a shock through Jean's body. This was Sienna's grandfather. Her *grandfather,* who apparently loves trains and busses as much as she does. Jean had been so consumed with the fact that Sienna was going to meet Maya that she didn't think for a moment about Kai and Sandy.

Wynn noticed the deer-in-the-headlights look on Jean's face and interjected, "So, where is Maya?"

"She's in the pool. Come on, you have to check it out! Do you like to swim?" Kai asked Sienna. Sienna said yes and took Kai's hand in eager anticipation. Even in her frazzled state, Jean had to admit that stepping into this crazy dome house was a treat. The entryway was simply majestic. The huge, arched ceiling above them was painted a pale blue that matched multi-colored mosaic tiles in the floor. There were tall, tropical-looking plants (maybe a banana tree?) on either side of the entrance, completing the Mediterranean feel. To their right was a staircase covered in some sort of Persian carpet that twisted up the curved walls to a second floor. In front of them was an arched entryway to what looked like an open kitchen/living space, with built-in alcoves covered in Moroccan pillows, but they were not headed that way. Kai and Sienna, who was stepping very carefully to avoid touching the grout lines between the mosaic tiles, were already walking out a patio door to their left. Wynn and Jean looked at each other and Wynn gave a reassuring smile and pantomimed taking a deep breath. Jean gulped a little air and followed.

Outside on a redwood deck, Jean was confronted with the same fantastic view they'd had in the parking area. To her left there was a wall of bamboo providing privacy from the cars, and maybe a windbreak. In front of her was a large pool sunk into the deck. The edge was infinity-style so that it looked as though you could just swim right out into that huge expanse of air.

On the far side of the deck was an outdoor barbecue kitchen and a large picnic table. An image of the wealthy ex-Dead Heads and their wives, wearing colorful, flowing silk tops and locally made jewelry, grilling California oysters with this view flashed through Jean's mind. A few steps down from the deck was a sandy area with a fire pit, and two palm trees perfectly situated to support a white woven hammock. Just to complete the picture of serenity, somebody was lying on the hammock. It looked like Sandy, from what Jean could remember of her.

"They call it hydro-therapy," Kai explained. "The PT wants her to get in the pool every day to keep up her strength. It doesn't put too much pressure on her leg." And there she was. Maya swimming underwater in the pool, her long, dark hair fanning out behind her. "That's why she's coming back to

Peru with us, plenty of hydro-therapy there!" Kai prattled on, but Jean stopped listening to him. Maya had noticed them and was swimming over.

"Hi! I'm so glad you could make it. Jesse told me that you might come today," said Maya, presumably to Jean, but she was staring at Sienna. "I'm Maya," she said, putting her wet hand out to shake Sienna's.

"Are you a mermaid?" Sienna asked.

"No, but I can swim like one," Maya answered, and then ducked underwater and swam in a circle, undulating her body like the mythical creature. When she turned, Jean could see a red scar along her spine, but her legs were too deep in the water to see the missing foot, or actually, not see it.

"I'm going to be a mermaid when I grow up," Sienna announced when Maya popped back up.

Jean decided to interrupt. "Um, yeah, Jesse said you were leaving town. I thought we'd stop by for an hour..." Jean said, reflexively limiting Maya's time with Sienna, but knowing that it was ridiculous to drive a four-hour round trip for a one-hour visit. Even if Jean wanted to leave after an hour, it would be cruel to put the kids back in the car so soon.

"...or so..." Jean added and then, perhaps sensing the tension in the air, Arvin chose that moment to wake up with a wail, startling everyone. Jean took the carrier from Wynn and pulled him out of the seat. Poor thing, his hair was matted with sweat. Jean had overdressed him. She pulled off his little jacket and looked around for somewhere to sit, because her breast was the only thing that would stop his howling. Her breasts knew it too; she could already feel tingling bolts of lightning spreading through them as they prepared to let down. "Excuse me, the baby...." she mumbled and turned to take the little screamer over to a lounge chair. Actually, she felt relieved to have an excuse to walk away for a moment and catch her breath.

Sienna followed Jean, leaving Wynn alone to chat with Maya and Kai. I am definitely paying for her to do a spa day after this, Jean decided. There was no way I could have done today without Wynn. "NuNee, can I go swimming?" Sienna asked. "I'm feeling hot." Before Jean could answer, Sienna started to take off her long-sleeved Hello Kitty shirt. It had been foggy in Santa Cruz that morning. Jean scolded herself for not realizing that it would be warm way up here. She didn't think to bring sunscreen or towels or anything.

"I'm sorry, sweetie, we didn't bring your suit. I didn't know there would be a pool..." Jean said, knowing full well that this was going to be a battle. "Why don't you play in the sand? You could build a sandcastle?"

"No! I want to swim!" Sienna said, already in pout mode and pulling down her skirt. Jean was about to chastise her with some empty threat about leaving if she couldn't be a good listener when Kai yelled over, "Come swim, Sienna! No suits needed here!" Sienna took off before Jean could say anything and she sat, abandoned except for little Arvin, who was passionately nursing a breast bigger than his head. "She doesn't know how!" Jean yelled over to Kai, but she knew this was a losing battle. Sienna was a total water baby and *would* eventually get in the pool.

"Don't worry, I've got her!" yelled Maya, as Sienna ripped off the last of her clothing and flung herself into the deep end of the pool. Jean cringed but stayed put. She was in no position to dive into the pool at that moment and, she thought, if this is happening, I guess I need to let it happen. She looked at her watch. Five minutes and counting. Maya caught Sienna and spun her in a big circle. Sienna's squeals of joy rose into the sky. She wasn't a shy girl, but she was not always so quick to warm up to strangers. Could she somehow know they weren't strangers? Jean wondered.

"Again!" Sienna insisted and Maya complied, swirls of water spinning outwards from their bodies as they twirled around. She must be hopping on one foot down there, Jean noted. Sienna had Maya's black hair and olive skin tone. Any fool would know that they were related.

"May I sit down?" Sandy's voice startled Jean.

"Wow, I guess the deck boards are screwed on tightly. I didn't hear you approaching me." Jean nodded toward the space next to her on the lounger, which she was sitting cross-wise on so she could nurse Arvin upright.

"How old is he?" Sandy asked the perennial opening question between mothers, who so clearly remember the vast differences between stages.

Sleeping for hours at a time at six days? Screaming for hours at a time at six weeks? Sleep smiling or wake smiling? Still giving you hickies around your breasts, or is he latching his mouth to your nipple as well as he instinctively knew to latch his hand to yours? Just then Arvin popped off and looked up at Jean with milk drooling out of his mouth before returning to the matter at hand.

"Oh! So cute! He's checking you out," Sandy cooed. She was wearing her graying hair in two long braids that went halfway down her back, and a long blue Mumu-type dress that did little to conceal the fact that she wasn't wearing a bra. She must be older than Kai, and didn't have his kinetic energy or his charming glow. Also, while Kai was classically handsome: tall, thin, blond, with a strong jawline; Sandy was what they call "pleasantly plump," with dark hair and a strong ethnic (perhaps Jewish?) nose.

Jean glanced over at Kai, who was talking excitedly to Wynn about something or other, his arms moving about wildly as he gestured with his hands. Four years ago when Maya was pregnant, Kai made an impression, but Jean hardly noticed Sandy. Back then Jean was a young, energetic thirty-four-year-old woman with still-perky titties and a gym-honed body. Now Jean was a tired thirty-eight-year-old mother of two small children, and Sandy's calm, easy-going vibe was definitely a better fit.

"Five weeks. I think he's just starting to notice that I'm always around when he's eating," Jean said, looking down at her happy little bundle. "Like,

'Hey! Weren't you here last time?'"

"He's going to get a lot of attention with those eyes!" Sandy said with a warm laugh, while petting Arvin's little bald head with her finger. Arvin had big blue eyes which were set off by skin so fair it looked ethereal. He was born with a copper fuzz on his head, but it had been mostly rubbed off by his bedding, so there were no other colors to compete with those liquid eyes. Jean had taken to calling him her little moon face.

Jean had mostly stayed home since Arvin was born, working from her home office, but the few times they'd ventured out, several people had stopped them to comment on his eyes. Maverick had the same blue eyes, which were from Marvin's side of the family. Sienna and Jean were both brown-eyed and, actually, it annoyed Jean a little that people were so obsessed with blue eyes. Who decided that blue and green were the best colors for eyes? But they fit Arvin, who at five weeks old was already so different from his sister. Where Sienna was born with the strong, thick body Maya obviously inherited from Sandy, Arvin felt delicate, and already looked like he would have Marvin's wiry frame.

The splashing from the pool distracted her. "Is Maya strong enough to be swinging Sienna around the pool like that? I didn't have a chance to warn Sienna that Maya was injured and she is not, by nature, a gentle girl." Jean didn't want to seem rude, but if Maya couldn't walk, how would she be able to keep up with Sienna's love of roughhousing?

"Don't worry. Maya is tough. She's doing really well getting used to the cane, and they've already had her practicing on a temporary prosthetic. And she's great in the water. Whenever she came home from college she taught swim lessons to the local niños," Sandy assured Jean, leaning back against the cushion to further relax her body into this gorgeous day. Jean looked over at Maya and imagined her playing with other mothers' children while Jean cared for her child. She and Sienna were laughing about the farty noises their lips make while blowing bubbles. The water looked cool and fresh. Jean wondered if the no bathing suit rule applied to grownups as well.

They heard a car pull up and a few minutes later, Jesse emerged from the house. "I bought chicken and portabella mushrooms for dinner, I hope that's okay with everyone. I thought we should take advantage of this grill," he said, then he looked at Jean. "Hi, Jean! How do you like the Hippy Fruition?"

"It suits me perfectly, Jesse," Jean said, and then realized that it was true. The big ball of fear she'd had in her stomach for weeks anticipating this moment had melted. "Thank you for encouraging me to come."

"I hope you can stay for dinner, Jean. Jesse got enough groceries to last us a few days so I know there's plenty. You should see the sunset from here. Absolutely amazing. We'd love it if you stayed the night, even. One room up there has four bunk beds. You wouldn't need anything," Sandy said.

"Oh, well, I'm sure it's fabulous, but, um, I'll have to check with Wynn. She has two children at home who are expecting dinner themselves." They had told Wynn's husband they'd be home around six. Jean looked at her watch; it was already after two. They would have to leave by four to make it back in time. "It's a big deal for Wynn to be away from her kids all day so I know she has to get back."

"NuNee!" Sienna called out, "NuNee! I need a towel."

"Okay, sweetie!" Jean responded, and then looked at Sandy. "Do you have any towels? I didn't know there was going to be a pool."

"No problem," she assured her, then yelled toward the house, "Jesse! Will you grab a towel for Sienna?" Jesse didn't answer immediately, so Sandy got up to go inside. Just as she got to the door Jesse, who had changed into a bathing suit himself, appeared with an armload of colorful beach towels.

"I'm on it," he reassured Sandy. "Towel delivery!" Wynn leaned over and helped Sienna out of the pool, wrapping her in a towel. Then she picked her up and walked over to Jean.

"Taco delivery!" Wynn joked, and plopped Sienna down in the spot Sandy had vacated.

Sienna cuddled up to Jean and said, "NuNee, I'm hungry. What snacks did you bring?" Jean reached over and opened the zipper on the diaper bag. She always brought snacks. Providing snacks gave Jean the feeling of being connected to some ancient vein of mothers, generations and generations of women feeding their young. Jean loved the feeling so much you'd think she would put more effort into dinners, but she got her ancient mother kick with snacks. Marvin was the real cook at their house.

"There are apple slices and crackers with cheese in here. And, I brought juice boxes," Jean said, knowing that Sienna would delight in the special treat. She usually only got juice boxes at other children's birthday parties, but Jean was fully prepared to bribe her today. Sienna dug in the bag and then carefully set up a picnic for them.

Looking at her sweet daughter lovingly offer her a cracker/apple/cheese/cracker sandwich, Jean felt embarrassed about the bag of Skittles she had stashed in her jacket. She'd bought them yesterday in a moment of total panic. As if her daughter, who she has loved from birth, who still climbed into her bed most nights even though all she got to cuddle with was Jean's back while she nursed Arvin, who loved her more than anyone else in the world, would fall so hard for a stranger that Jean needed sugar to get her to agree to come home. *What a fool I am!* Jean looked over at Maya, who traveled across the country to create a relationship with Sienna and almost died. Who had been here for weeks while Jean stalled. Who was leaving for Peru in a matter of days. Who was, whether Jean liked it or not, part of Sienna's family.

"Wahoo!" Jesse yelled as he cannonballed into the

deep end of the pool. Then Kai stripped off his shorts and dove in too. His lack of tan line didn't surprise Jean, but she couldn't help noticing that his penis looked small. Figures. Sienna giggled and ran back to the pool, her little round butt bouncing. There are few things cuter in this world than a baby's bottom.

"Well, if I had known that this was a nudist pool party I would have brought my pre-baby body," Wynn joked.

"Yeah, sorry, Jesse didn't say anything about a pool on the telephone."

"How are you doing? You look relaxed," Wynn noted.

"You know, I'm feeling dumb. I cannot believe that I was so worried about this. Thanks so much for talking me into coming, Wynn," Jean said. "I really owe you."

"No problem, Jean. You were so stressed about this the past couple of months. I just knew the mountain would shrink to a molehill once you actually faced it. Or, at least, I was hoping it would!"

"Yeah, I guess those damned pregnancy hormones really worked me," Jean said, feeling sheepish. She had really leaned on Wynn these past months. Wynn probably thought that getting her to just drive over here and deal with it was the only way to shut her up.

"Speaking of molehill..." Wynn indicated to Maya, who had climbed out of the pool and was now hobbling toward them with the cane, the sunlight glistening across its silver in little jagged streaks. The place where her foot should be was empty air. "I think Sandy is inside. Maybe I can get her to give me a tour of this insane house." Wynn excused herself and left Jean alone to talk with Maya.

"Thank you for coming. I thought maybe you weren't," Maya said after turning in a circle and slowly lowering herself down to sit next to Jean on the lounge chair.

"Well, Jesse insisted that this might be Sienna's last chance to meet you for a while."

"Yeah..." Maya's voice trailed off as her eyes watched Sienna playing with Jesse in the pool. Up close, Maya looked tired. Defeated, even. Jean remembered her being so spunky.

"Are you looking forward to going to Peru?" Jean asked, already knowing the answer. Twenty-two-year-olds don't want to move back in with their parents.

"I guess I couldn't go back to DC. It just doesn't make sense. I don't have anyone there to help me and, I don't know, I'd probably be all right. The doctors say that I will be walking on my own with a prosthetic. But my parents are dead-set against it." Jean looked at Maya struggle with this decision and her dad's cockamamie plan to forego physical therapy.

"I wouldn't want Maverick hobbling around some far-off city by himself, either. How close are you to finishing college?" Maverick was a sophomore now, so Jean guessed that Maya was a junior if she went straight to college after high school.

"I have one year left. I was trying to get it done in three years to save money," she answered. According to Jean's calculations that means she took a year off between high school and college. She was a senior when she had Maya; maybe it took her a bit to get on with things.

"What were you studying?" Jean asked.

"Political science. I want to go into politics. Or maybe law. I guess I want to change the world as much as my parents do, but in a bigger way. They're building one house at a time down in Peru with Habitación. I want to change the ways governments run things so everyone can afford to own a home." Maya's eyes sparkled as she described her dream, but then the spark dissipated and, as if it took a great amount of energy to work up the shine in the first place, she looked even more exhausted. "Now I'll probably never graduate."

"Don't say that. I'm sure you'll go back. It sounds like you could even graduate with your class," Jean tried to reassure her. Everything seems so massive when you're young, but she'd bounce back. On the other hand, sometimes massive things happen, like car crashes and babies, and losing a foot, and your life is never the same again. Jean looked over at Arvin, who was lying in his carrier, sucking on the nose of a little stuffed monkey. She felt so blessed to have him, to have all three of her children. In fact,

Jean thought, I am lucky to have such a comfortable life: a kind husband, a humming law practice (that was somehow going to accommodate this new baby!), a beautiful home. And then Jean quickly shamed herself for thinking of these things while sitting next to someone who'd taken such a hit.

"My parents never wanted me to go to college in the first place. After we left Santa Cruz and moved down to Peru, they tried to get me to stay there and get a job with them at Habitación. It took a year before they finally agreed to let me go to college. I just don't have it in me to fight anymore. I don't know, maybe they're right. Family should stick together. I guess I'll do some online courses to finish up," she said. The word "family" rang in Jean's ears. Family: a group of people you did not choose, whom you may love or hate, who are cemented into your life. Not just your life, they are cemented into your very psyche, and there they remain, even if you never see them again.

"Do you have any other family in the States you could stay with while you complete college?" Jean asked. There had to be someone.

"No, my aunt Jude lives in Iowa where Dad grew up, but she and Dad are not on great terms, and my mom grew up in the foster care system. She only has us. We've always been the three musketeers." Maya clenched her fists and did a marching motion with her arms when she repeated the term that probably felt so secure when she was a child and so suffocating now. "Not that I'm complaining. I love my parents. They've been amazing these past weeks taking care of me."

"What about Jesse?" Jean asked realizing that she'd been assuming that he was Maya's boyfriend without really knowing what his story was.

Maya smiled. "We're just friends. I met him at the beginning of the summer. He felt so familiar, at first I thought that I was interested in him romantically, but then I knew I wasn't. Still, he felt so comfortable, like family, even when we argued. It wasn't until after my parents showed up that I realized the reason why he feels so familiar to me is because my parents have always had one or two guys like him around. My dad is a great carpenter, and ever since I was a child he's built houses for rich eccentrics. He built most of this house; that's why we're staying here. Because they're such mainstream dropouts themselves, they like to take runaways under their wings. We always had one or two guys his type camping in our backyard or garage. Ostensibly they trade their 'labor' for a place to stay, but really my dad was teaching them a skill while my mom warms them up with mom-love. I still think of a few of them as big brothers, but I wouldn't go live with any of them."

"Wow, I had no idea that Kai built this house," Jean said, impressed. She was even more impressed that he didn't say anything. Could she have the wrong impression of that guy? One of these days, Jean thought, I'm just going to give up on judging people. She looked over at Jesse swinging Sienna around in the pool. Without his punk clothes on he looked like a normal kid, except for that metal sticking out of his nostrils. "So, is Jesse going to help them build something?"

"Oh, I don't know. I guess right now he's here helping me build something..." Maya looked away from Jean for a moment and when she turned back there were tears in her eyes. "I know you wouldn't have come if he hadn't called you. Jean, I'm so glad you came. I wanted to call you myself, but I've been depressed over everything. I just had the feeling that you and Sienna wouldn't want to see me and, I'm sorry. It's all so awkward. And I couldn't just blame the crash. I've wanted to call you for years. I wanted to see her, but I was afraid she would hate me for leaving her, or for coming back, or both. When Jesse showed up, I don't know, I felt brave for a moment. But then the crash just took it out of me. I didn't know what to do."

Jean didn't know what to do either, but she couldn't help but recognize Maya's pain and confusion: it was mother guilt, classic case. "Like, where is the handbook for this shit, right?" Jean offered. There were a lot of handbooks Jean would like to get her paws on. Where was the handbook for fulfilling the needs of your older children when you have a new baby? Where was the handbook for trying to have a career and be a mother with the same body? Jean looked at Maya, who had put her head in her hands. Where was the handbook on how to deal with this broken bird who had all the love of a mother and, yet, still needed a mother? Not so long ago it was Jean who was a teen mom, going to college while her mother cared for her baby. The difference was that Jean got to come home every night and parent him too. If her mother hadn't been such a support, maybe Jean would have had to give Maverick up like Maya did. And Maverick loves his grandmother, at least as much as he loves Jean. Maybe more. And, come to think of it, Jean had never felt jealous of that divided love. A child's love naturally expands to encompass any person in his family that loves him.

Jean thought of Kai and Sandy making family out of those young men that stumbled onto their paths along the way. If they can do that, surely Jean could make a friend out of her daughter's family member. "Do you think Jesse would be willing to drive Sienna and me back to Santa Cruz tomorrow?"

CHAPTER NINETEEN

"LET ME TELL you about love," Kai said, with one hand digging in the built-in wooden cooler for another beer. "When I was a young, swinging bachelor, I had the best line in the business."

Jesse looked over at Maya, who was groaning and rolling her eyes at her dad, obviously embarrassed. This should be interesting.

"I'd go up to a promising young filly," he went on, "and say 'you know I can tell within ten minutes whether or not I'll fall in love with someone.' It worked, you see, because the girl felt challenged, and the challenge of winning temporally distracted her from deciding whether or not *I* was worth *her* time. The challenge was worth her time."

"So, that's how you got Sandy?" Jesse asked.

"Ha! That's how Sandy got me! Sandy won my

heart forever more with her response to my stupid line—"

"I think it was something like, 'wow, that's impressive! I can't tell if I love a man unless I feel comfortable shitting while he's in the shower!'" Sandy laughed at the memory. "You should have seen the look on his face!"

"That was the look of pure love, baby." Kai squeezed his wife closer.

Jean walked out the sliding glass door and carefully closed it behind her. From where Jesse was sitting, he could see that she'd put Sienna to sleep in the living room window seat, probably to keep her in sight. Jean sat down on a teak Adirondack chair next to where Maya was lying on an old quilt with baby Arvin, but she didn't take the baby. Arvin looked super comfortable all cuddled up in Maya's arms. Jesse jabbed a stick into the fire Kai and he had built, sending a swirl of lit embers into the smoke. It was a beautiful, clear night and the five—six if you included Arvin—of them were circled around the fire pit like old friends. Even though this was some posh retreat house in the Berkeley Hills, not the countryside in Virginia, the fire pit reminded him of an annual Boy Scout camping trip he used to go on in Shenandoah. Jesse leaned back in his chair and looked around at the faces lit by the fire. What he had here were new friends, the silver variety in the old song. A silver lining of friendship on this crazy summer.

"Okay, everyone, let's play two truths and a lie,"

said Kai, as he twisted the cap off of his beer.

"That's where everyone takes turns telling three things; two of them true, and one of them a lie," explained Maya to Jesse's confused face. "I'll go first, you'll get it. Oh, and if you know the answer because you know the person who is saying it too well, you have to keep quiet. This is a get-to-know you game," she instructed, then began, "Not to brag, but I was at the top of my class in eighth grade, twelfth grade, and freshman year in college."

"Wow," said Jean, "two of those are true? Impressive."

"You have to guess which is the lie," reminded Maya.

"I'm guessing eighth grade is the lie," Jesse offered. "I don't think that they kept track of that in my middle school."

"I'm going with college, just to have a different guess," said Jean, looking over at Maya's parents.

"Don't look at me!" Kai said. "As far as I can remember, my brilliant daughter has always been at the top of her class."

"You're both wrong! I came in second in my class in twelfth grade." Maya laughed. "Now you see how to play. It's really a game of self-promotion. Your turn, Jesse."

"Hmm...okay...my favorite authors are Steinbeck, Kerouac, and Burroughs."

"No fair, Jesse, one of them has to be a lie," Maya said.

"Okay, I was going to say that I like Burroughs

less, but it isn't a total lie. Hmm, okay, here's one. I have jumped out of a plane, skied down a slope, and rafted a river."

"I'm guessing that you have never jumped out of a plane," said Sandy. "I think you paused a little longer before saying that one."

"Ooh, tricky, tricky! I think it was the skiing. I've skied for years and I've never heard of anyone saying 'skied a slope' before—you usually just say 'skied'," said Kai, making his voice all formal when saying "skied a slope."

"Ha, you're right, Kai! I've never been skiing."

"Wow, you really jumped out of a plane?" asked Jean, looking impressed again.

"Yeah, on my eighteenth birthday. A few friends and I did it together," Jesse explained, thinking of how awkward it was to have that big, hairy instructor strapped to his back tandem-style the whole way down, penis pressed to ass. Actually, maybe it wasn't that awkward.

"Okay, my turn," said Sandy. "I've loved a Peruvian man while traveling in Belize, a French man while traveling in Thailand, and a Japanese man while living in Hawaii."

"Mom!" said Maya in a tone Jesse imagined she'd used throughout much of her childhood. No wonder she was trying so hard to be straight: excelling in school, going to college in DC. Jesse thought hippy parents would be a dream, and certainly Maya's life sounded like an epilogue to the best beat novel, but he was starting to get why Maya was obviously a little embarrassed of her dope-smoking, dreadlocked dad and overtly sensual (sexual) mom.

"Oh, we're all adults here, Maya," dismissed Kai before turning to his wife to protest. "What about my white butt in Peru?" But the look in his eyes was pride, not jealousy.

"Hmm... I guess this is up to Jesse and me to figure out. You all obviously know the answer," said Jean, who didn't seem at all unnerved by this freaky family. Jesse thought of Utah Phillips, an old-time folk singer popularized by Ani Defranco, said that you have to have an open mind if you live in California; if you don't, they'll pry it open for you. Or something like that. Jesse's ex-girlfriend had played the album, and Jesse always liked that line. Even though Jean looked like any suburban mom back in Virginia, she was still Californian.

"I remember that Maya spent part of her childhood in Hawaii, and you live somewhat close to Belize now, so I'm guessing that the French man in Thailand is a lie," Jean deduced.

Sandy didn't blink. She was probably good at poker. Jesse was admittedly terrible at poker, his whole body shaking with the excitement of trying to bluff. Right now he was doing his best to bluff that he fit in with this crowd. That this was all totally cool with him. That he wasn't thinking what he was thinking: How many different men had Sandy had sex with? How was it that Kai didn't mind? Did he watch, or did he just go out and do his own thing when she was doing hers? Jesse's upbringing had not prepared him to even fathom how a relationship like this worked, but neither did Kai's Midwestern childhood. It was one thing to step out of the rushing mainstream, and an entirely different thing to subvert the dominant paradigm of your ego. Yet, here he was: calmly joking about his wife's lovers. Jesse felt like he was getting a peek into a different universe, a universe where the rules of physics don't apply, where you get to define your own cosmology. He wanted to go to the University of Kai and Sandy, learn their secret for finding the route to Self, then use the tools to build the foundation of his own universe. "Just to be different, I am going to guess the Japanese guy is the lie."

"You're both wrong!" Sandy laughed. "I've only been with my darling Kai in Belize," she said, reaching over and giving her husband a little squeeze. "Your turn, Jean."

"Okay, um, to relax I take Valium, marijuana, and bubble baths," said Jean.

"Bubble baths was definitely the lie," Jesse joked.

"It's obvious, Valium is the lie," said Sandy, and Kai nodded his head too.

"Hmm...then just to guess differently, I'm going to say no weed," said Maya.

"You were right," Jean said to Sandy and Kai. "I've never tried Valium, but there is nothing like a soak and smoke to cool down a mom's nerves."

"I was hoping you would say that!" Kai exclaimed and then promptly pulled out his quickly waning weed stash to roll a joint, but then added, "don't worry I'll save this for later when I'm not around the baby."

"You don't strike me as the type that gets stressed out easily," said Maya. Jesse kept quiet, but he knew Maya was wrong about that. He hasn't spent much time with the woman, but he could recognize a fellow head spinning neurotic when he saw one. Jean did appear calmer now then when she first showed up earlier in the afternoon. Actually, Jesse reflected, being around the Barsky family caused him to feel calmer as well. Something about how easily they all seemed to accept themselves gave Jesse permission to accept himself as well.

"You know, I don't feel so stressed at the moment, but believe me... I have my days," Jean laughed, obviously not ready to admit that this day started out as one of those days.

"It's the Barsky effect, Jean," Jesse said.

"Yes," "hanging with us is like existing inside the purple haze," joked Kai waving his hands around as if he were mesmerizing the group. Everyone laughed.

"No, really, I'm serious," Jesse said, "You guys are good for soothing anxiety. Jean and I are lucky to be a part of this," he said, expanding his hands to include the fire, the company, the luxurious deck, and the crisp, clear night sky. Then he looked at Jean, wanting her to see the truth in his statement, realizing that he wanted her to accept Maya. Jean had the chance to be a part of this family.

"You're right Jesse. I was so worried about how

everything would go today and now I'm glad I came. Thank you Barsky for this lovely night." Jean was looking at Maya, who hadn't moved from the blanket on the sand because Arvin was still sleeping soundly. He felt good about the effort he'd put in to convince Jean to visit and he knew he wouldn't stop until Jean accepted Maya, he would do it for Maya and he would do it because it was right.

"Well, we are lucky to have you, too!" said Sandy, giving them a loving, happy smile.

"So, the lawyer likes to get a little stony" Kai said, focusing on rolling his joint into a perfect cylinder so intently he was missing the love fest.

"Yeah, you don't strike me as the weed type," Jesse couldn't help but say. She looked like the opposite of the weed type to him.

"You have a lot to learn about the weed type, young man." Jean laughed. "I've been an occasional smoker since high school."

"Oh, really?! Wild party girl, huh?" Kai teased.

"Well, I wouldn't go so far as that! Except I did have Maverick at 17," she replied. Jesse looked over at Jean, he knew about Maverick, obviously, but he hadn't put it together before that Jean was a teen mom just like Maya.

"So the wild party girl got knocked up," teased Kai, who didn't seem too worried about insulting Jean. Maybe in his world being a knocked-up wild party girl was a good thing.

"So, what was your excuse, Maya? You're hardly the wild party girl," Jesse asked, genuinely curious.

Maya was the opposite of the out-of-control party girl. She had also insisted on protection every time they had sex.

"Broken condom," Maya explained. "And don't act like I'm a total prude. I met you in a club," she said, defensively poking Jesse in the chest.

"Aww...broken condom...that's what they all say," joked Kai, but in his daughter's case he should probably have believed it.

"I didn't know you two met in a club," interjected Sandy. "I'm so glad that you're getting out there and playing a little, Maya." She then turned to Jean. "Maya gets so serious about her studies. I try to warn her that the golden apple those college people hold out for you is really made of tin, but she won't listen to her old mom."

"Yes, we tell our daughter: if you follow the herd, you end up an unhappy cow. Does she listen? Of course, I'm the last person to argue that a child should always follow in her parents' footsteps. If I'd listened to mine I'd be applying for middle management in my dad's construction business back in Ohio right now." Kai shook his sun-bleached dreadlocks in mock horror, like middle management was a life sentence.

"Oh, I don't think that a political science degree at George Washington is following the herd so much," Jean said, rising to Maya's defense. "Anyway, the mainstream needs fresh energy with creative minds." Jean and Maya looked at each other. To Jesse they seemed really similar. It was like they were two willow trees on the edge of a river: digging their roots into conventionalism while the splendid chaos of California's exceptionalism swirled all around. Before now, he had never imagined that someone would choose to be part of mundane society. He just figured most people were sheeple, moving along, eating grass, without further analysis. And yet, here was Maya, who went to college instead of being a hippy on the beach in Peru. Here was Jean, who decided to be a lawyer in Northern California. Two people who, if they had followed the mainstream in the place they grew up in, would never have chosen the paths they chose. Maybe convincing Jean to accept Maya as family wouldn't be too hard.

"Ain't that the truth!" agreed Kai, raising his beer. "To my brilliant daughter learning the Man's tools to take down the Man's house!"

"To creative minds finding their own path in life," corrected Sandy, smiling at her daughter, the warm firelight giving her soft, round face an especially loving, maternal glow. And to that they all cheered.

CHAPTER TWENTY

MAVERICK HAD THAT tall, ruddy, California surfer-look with a mouth full of perfect white teeth that gleamed at you through an adorable, slightly crooked smile. Plus, he took care of sick puppies for a living. Jesse was not in the least surprised that Maya got herself knocked up. If Maverick were inclined, Jesse would get knocked up, too. Basking in the not so faded glory of his high school popularity, he was holding court at the nightclub. Santa Cruz must really be a small town because Maverick knew everyone there. Girls were swooning, and one of them actually stepped on Jesse's toe trying to squeeze closer to get his attention.

Jesse might have hated Maverick except, not only was he gorgeous, he was drippingly, almost salesman-nice. In the social food chain the people at the very top and very bottom were often kind, something about their position being locked in created enough stability to be generous. The people you have to be aware of are the active climbers. People who lost their footing and would step on you to reach higher ground. Maverick clearly had a strong hold at the top, with plenty of room to be generous. He kept introducing Jesse to his old friends, as if any one of them gave a rat's ass, and he even got his buddy behind the bar to give Jesse discounts on beer.

Jesse had met Maverick when he drove Jean home a few days before and the guy had practically forced him to agree to return to see this "amazing" local cover band. The band was actually pretty good for a bunch of white dudes playing reggae. Not that Jesse was any great connoisseur, but "Redemption Song" does look a little funny when everyone but the keyboardist is white.

The crowd was mostly twenty-somethings wearing clothes that were several degrees more casual than what people wear in DC clubs. Back home, whether your style was punk or prep, you always checked the mirror before leaving home. Of course it was a reggae band, but most of the crowd looked to Jesse like they were three days into a no-shower reggae festival instead of just out for the night. Standing beside him at the bar, a tan surfer-type with beautiful, long blond hair was flirting with a hippy girl who was wearing one of those pre-torn shirts—Jesse estimated he could rip the rest off with his pinky—the type that looked homemade, but she probably paid top dollar for it.

Mr. California, who was wearing surf shorts and flip-flops even though they were in a night club not on a beach, was saying something about how the feminine moon reflects the masculine light of the sun. Jesse was fairly certain that that line would just piss off any girl he was trying to pick up. Maya, for example, would probably vomit and run. But the girl with the pre-shredded clothes looked entranced. If you look like the sun god himself, it doesn't matter what kind of diarrhea you spew out of your mouth, Jesse thought grimly. Then he thought he should work on his tan.

That was, if he didn't go back to Virginia. Right after the accident, Jesse had been so busy with his guilt and the moment-to-moment needs of Maya's daily therapy schedule, he completely gave up on his California adventure plans and was almost looking forward to retreating to his old bedroom in Reston, Virginia the moment the Barskys said something, anything, that would allow him to gracefully leave. But they hadn't and he felt so guilty about the accident, about the *loss of Maya's foot*, that he could hardly excuse himself.

For the first week or so he kept expecting them to say something along the lines of "we're here now, we'll take care of Maya, you should go home," or maybe pull him aside to scream at him for harming their daughter, to kick him out and tell him never to call. Instead they just seemed to merrily act as if he was part of the family, as if he had always been part of the family, and it would never occur to them that he would go anywhere else. So, he went berry picking with Sandy for Kai's famous blackberry crumble. He went up on the roof of the Hippy Fruition with Kai and helped repair some shingles. He drove Maya to physical therapy and, suddenly, weeks had gone by.

While he and Sandy were picking blackberries a few days earlier, Sandy delighting in the sweet taste and the warm sun with the innocence of a sage, Jesse had the revelation that the reason why he and Maya didn't work out was because he mistook her for her mother thirty years earlier. Not that he wanted to do Sandy—even as a self-proclaimed sexual omnivore she was 20 years and at least 100 pounds away from being what he wanted to fuck—but that he was more similar to Sandy and Kai than he was to Maya. They grew up in normal, civilized life and broke free. While their childhood friends worked nine to five and saved up for the white picket fence, Sandy and Kai renamed themselves after the place where the ocean hit the shore and dove into the wilds. They forged their own truth, and will never be forced to conform themselves back into the small mind of middle America.

Jesse thought Maya would be his launching partner, but Maya never chose the life Kai and Sandy led. The one that Jesse wanted. She was born into that swirl of free spirit and Jesse could see now that, although her hippy heritage kept her somewhat exotic—she would always feel comfortable stripping her clothes off at a hot spring and debating the merits of GMO food—she'd do the career and picket fence life, not the carefree traveling life.

Jesse had all but given up on his own plans for adventure after the accident. Not that there wasn't any discussion about the future at the Hippy Fruition. It just wasn't his future that was discussed so intently around the dinner table. The more Kai and Sandy kept talking to Maya about returning with them to Peru, the more resigned Maya seemed to her fate. She admitted that she couldn't return to her DC life yet, she needed family around her while she learned to live with her loss, but she wasn't happy.

Jesse had heard Maya talking to Jean about it all on the phone a couple days after Jean had stayed the night. Jesse had pestered Jean the whole way home about letting Maya have a second visit with Sienna before she left. He told her that she needed to be the one to call Maya, that Maya was usually quite confident and unafraid to take up space, but her accident had brought her low. That she needed a reason to keep fighting to stay on her own path instead of her parent's. When Jean called Maya to make plans for the visit they ended up talking for over an hour about Maya's future and Maya's fears that her dreams would be delayed if she didn't finish her college degree.

When Maya got off the telephone she seemed a little less depressed, but later her mood plummeted again and she cried to Jesse that she felt like once she was settled in Peru she would be so far away from Sienna it would be years before the next visit.

Without really thinking of it, Jesse had assumed that eventually the Barskys would announce they were leaving and he would head back to Virginia. Until this morning. At breakfast Kai started talking about his work building houses for Habitación, about how it had programs all around the world and how, after Maya fully recovered, he and Sandy would be moving down to Uruguay for a few years to assist with the launch in that country. And then, Jesse felt certain, but could definitely have misheard, that Kai seemed to assume Jesse would be accompanying them to Peru. He was talking about what a smart program it was, charging wealthy Americans thousands of dollars to build houses for the poor around the world. Then, Jesse could swear Kai said, "Of course, you'd be working with me, so you're not an official volunteer and don't have to pay." Or maybe he said, "Of course, *if* you're working with me you're not an official volunteer and don't have to pay." Jesse got so flooded with emotion at the idea of traveling to Peru, either excitement or fear, but definitely panic, that even seconds afterward he couldn't recall exactly which it was.

Not knowing what to say, Jesse said something like, "Oh shit! I forgot I was supposed to call my friend," and then ran to the bathroom to breathe for ten minutes and think. His mind was still swirling.

Did Kai invite him to Peru? Did he want to go to Peru? Under any other circumstance the answer would be: "Hell yes!" Of course he wanted to travel to exotic lands, eat foreign food, kiss brown skin. But didn't he, really, want to get away from Maya and his guilt? And didn't they realize by now that he wasn't her boyfriend? What, exactly, did they want with him? To confront his guilt on a daily basis forever more? Certainly, he deserved that. Or were they offering him a method of atonement? Could building houses under the hot Peruvian sun sweat out his crime?

Jesse looked around at these pale-skinned partiers with their dreadlocks and earth tones. He could imagine Kai and Sandy here as a young couple. Sandy swaying with her eyes closed, and Kai attracting even more attention than Maverick was tonight. Maya, who lived in the mind instead of the heart, would be bored. Jesse thought about how she was so upset that her parents were "forcing" her to go recuperate on the beach in Peru instead of allowing her to return to some stuffy college classroom. Maybe rather than hate him for almost killing their daughter, they saw Jesse as the child that they could relate to.

Certainly Jesse felt that he could relate to Kai and Sandy and it wasn't just because he had always wanted to be as cool as they were. In fact, Jesse realized that these past few weeks had mostly eradicated his age-old anxiety about how cool he was. His guilt had exhausted his self-esteem to the point where he'd lost his drive to try for coolness and, yet, helping Maya and her parents had built up something else where that hunger used to reside.

He had reverted to his old, boring, reliable self, helping Maya after the accident, the self that he'd wanted to finally shed by coming on this road trip in the first place, but if he had been the egocentric hedonist he'd idealized and was starting to become then he would never have gotten to know Kai and Sandy, never proven himself to them. Too afraid to attempt San Francisco on his own, he would have scurried back to DC and wasted several more years wishing he had the nerve to be the person he wanted to be, never having a clear idea of who that was. But that isn't how it went because that wasn't him, Jesse realized with pride. Like Kai, who took that job framing houses to support his wife while she healed from abuse, Jesse was the type of guy that can have fun, but be there for you in a crisis, take responsibility for his actions and do the right thing even when it's a hassle. It wasn't just that he was reliable, what he gained is the inner calm of someone that knows he can rely upon himself. Rather than a few wild fucks in San Francisco, he was fairly certain he had an invitation to build houses in Peru—the start of a true adventure. He was also fairly certain that he had the nerve to accept it.

CHAPTER TWENTY-ONE

SIENNA WAS DISAPPOINTED. She had been certain, and Jean guessed it was their fault, that she would wake up taller on her fourth birthday. For weeks Maya, Marvin, and Jean had been telling her about what a big girl she was going to be. Four does seem significantly older than three. The truism about the days being long but the years being short had been ringing loudly in Jean's ears lately.

"I want to be big!" Sienna sobbed, tears dripping onto the golden locket she wore around her neck.

"But, honey, you are big enough. You're perfectly big." Jean switched Arvin to her left breast and tried to pull poor Sienna in close on her right side. She blamed herself for this whole fixation on being big. She had wanted to not make being "big" a thing with Sienna. She had tried to avoid calling her a "big girl" as a compliment. Being a child was such an important and fleeting time of life, Jean wanted Sienna to appreciate it. She knew far too well the hazards of trying to grow up too quickly. But, like so many fine parenting ideas, the good intentions evaporated in the necessity of the moment. Being "big" can be a powerful motivator for a child. And, as mothers of three-year-olds everywhere know, you need to use every trick in the book to get them to bend to your will.

They'd forgotten to mention that one's birthday was not a leap forward, but simply a marker: a reminder that for 365 days you've been traveling around the sun and were now in the same general location you were at birth. Other than the love and offerings from the people who celebrate your life, birthdays do not grace you with any special gift. Unfortunately, they'd overhyped the event, and now Sienna was such a miserable wreck Jean was thinking of canceling the birthday party.

Not that canceling the actual party would do much to change the festive chaos in this house, she smiled to herself.

Maya was dashing around, her prosthetic foot banging away at the floor like a woodpecker, showing her parents the bathrooms, clean towels, and other odds and ends they would need during their stay. She was giving them her bed because they couldn't really afford hotels on their Peruvian salaries. She had already set up a foam mat on the floor for herself. Maverick and Marvin were outside tying balloons to the swing set, filling the cooler with juice boxes, making sure the new gate round the pool was secure, and generally setting up for the big event.

They were running late because, after Maverick picked up Kai and Sandy at the San Jose airport last night, he and Kai had spent half the night at a concert and didn't wake up till noon (thanks to the blackout curtains Jean had installed in Sienna's room a year ago with fantasies of getting more sleep... But that was B.A., Before Arvin). Maverick had invited Maya to join them for the show, but she had passed so she could spend some quality time with her mom and have plenty of energy for today. Maya was sensible like that.

The three-bedroom bungalow was now officially packed. Jean didn't mind. She loved having Maverick home, of course, and she was actually looking forward to Kai and Sandy visiting. She wanted them to see how well Maya was doing. Maya was working as both Jean's nanny and legal clerk, coordinating the transfer of her credits to UC Santa Cruz, doing weekly physical therapy, volunteering as treasurer of the local Young Democrat Association, and generally getting around on that prosthetic like she was born with it. Once Jean invited her to move in with them, Maya fought her parents tooth and nail to make it happen. It was actually impressive to watch. Maya was a force to be reckoned with in an argument and, really, her parents didn't have a chance. Jean couldn't wait to see her in the courtroom someday.

It was a good decision, too. She fit into their household, and Santa Cruz, like a puzzle piece. She was the butter greasing both the mother and the career woman gears of Jean's life, so they could turn smoothly together. Frankly, Jean can't imagine how she was planning on pulling it all off by herself. The best part was that Maya seemed to feel the same way. Maya told Jean and Marvin the other night, after she put Sienna to sleep and Arvin had exhausted himself by screaming, that Santa Cruz felt more like home to her than any other place ever has. She was already talking about taking the Law School Admissions Test next spring and wanted Jean to break the news to Kai. She said he was generally opposed to the very existence of lawyers, but Jean has a feeling that even Kai has seen this coming.

Plus, what better way to spend the settlement money than graduate school? Of course, Kai might argue that Jesse has the right plan. He took his share (which was just a smidgen compared to Maya's— Jesse barely even got hurt, but Jean had pressed hard for as much money as she could get—both of these kids had been through a lot) and went to work building houses with Kai and Sandy down in Peru.

Jean thought of how Jesse spoke grandly about working for them for six months, doing good for the impoverished people of Peru, and then taking his backpack, a one-person tent, and his thumb pointed to the sky until his luck ran out. Jean had wanted to cover Maverick's ears as Jesse prattled on about making it all the way to Patagonia. Apparently, Kai and Sandy have a whole network of contacts, like a secret map to the hippy hangouts everywhere, that they'd agreed to share with him once he got down there and sweated a little laying out rooftops. With Kai and Sandy as his compass, Jesse had let his wanderlust soar.

Jean knew that Maya missed Jesse, even Jean missed him a little. Despite his weird clothes, piercings and adolescent fixation on living some romantic beat life, she had to admit that there was something special about Jesse. Maya had told her that it was Jesse who encouraged her to come to California after he found out about Sienna, even paid her way!

Plus, Jean would never have opened her heart to Maya, probably wouldn't have even gone to visit if Jesse had allowed her even a few days of peace about it. That boy was tenacious! Jean was with Maya the day Maya bought Jesse a good-bye present: a leather bound notebook for his private scribbling. For his public audience, Marvin helped Jesse set up a website called "Jesse's Road," where he blogs his travels. Jean couldn't help but notice that Maverick seemed a little too excited about Jesse's latest post, *The Tao of Machu Picchu*, but Maverick still had another year of school so Jean crossed her fingers; hopefully he wouldn't take off just yet. Anyway, Jean glanced over at Maya; Maverick may find a reason to stay. Except, Jean had seen the way Maverick looked at Jesse.

Something in Jesse's recent post stuck in Jean's mind, "An uncertain future is the wonder and terror of life. Embrace that truth or risk missing everything."

"Hey! Birthday girl! Where are you?! Come out here!" Marvin called from the yard and Sienna went running, shedding her fit as she left her mother's presence. Jean followed and gasped as what she saw. The men had tied over twenty balloons into a huge heart. "Maya! Sandy! You have got to see this!" Jean yelled back into the kitchen. They came out and stared at the balloon art, which was staked in the middle of the yard like a maypole. "Now," said Marvin, "Now that we are all here, I want to take a moment and hold hands around this heart."

"We've come here today to celebrate a very special girl," Marvin said in a big, dramatic voice, "who has brought us all together like this balloon, many happy hearts forming one big heart."

"Three cheers for Sienna!" Grampa Kai said.

"Hip hip hooray!" yelled Sienna's family.

ACKNOWLEDGMENTS

I cannot express enough thanks to my friends and family members, Barbara, Marissa, Liz, Anita, Miriam, Desirae, and Mirjam, who agreed to be early readers and whose insights helped shape the story and deepen the characters. Marissa and Liz, especially, gave me their valuable time and honesty trudging through several drafts with vigor and love. Much of the flavor of the book and consistency in things like eye coloring are directly attributable to them. The dull parts are all me. Deep appreciation goes to my caring, loving, and supportive spouse who told me I could write a novel and then did the dishes while I wrote (thanks Babe). And finally, a heart full of gratitude to my children who inspired much of this story and then had to suffer my absence while I worked on it.

ABOUT THE AUTHOR

Deep down in the secret hearts of wannabe writers everywhere there is a little flame of hope that if they were to ever find the time to write a novel it would be fabulous. A horrible side effect of taking the time to write is that you must face the rest of your life knowing exactly what kind of first novel you would write if you only had the time. And so does anyone else who bothers to read it. Publishing a first novel is similar to sending a child you wish you would have raised more properly off to college: you feel like that desperate dad in Hamlet shouting things like "neither a borrower nor a lender be" and "to thine own self be true" out the door. In times like these one must turn to an oracle for wisdom, so I recently knelt before my computer and googled "first novel." It turns out that many popular authors' first novels were written in a style that is different from the style for which they later became famous. It's, like, a thing. Therefore, I feel that I have been given permission by the Great Spirit of the Holy Web to hold on to the hope that if I ever find the time to write a second novel it has every chance of being superior to this one.

Made in the USA
San Bernardino, CA
20 May 2015